RED LINED

THE MALLET
BOOK 3

P A WILSON

Ebook ISBN: 978-1-990509-13-1
Paperback ISBN: 978-1-990509-14-8
Audio book ISBN:978-1-990509-15-5

FREE EBOOK

Claim your copy of Running the Game when you use the QR code below to sign up for my newsletter and cheer on Pen as she vies for a commission in the military.

1

S ofie stood, eyes closed and hand pressed against the wall, waiting for the vertigo she'd experienced every day since the operation to turn the room on its axis. A minute later, when nothing had happened, she dropped her hand. The surgeon had told her the dizziness would go away, but Sofie didn't believe she was free of it. She'd spent her whole life fearing that the Fades would attack at the wrong time — not that there was a right time. Trusting that her Fades were gone and it was all over would take some time.

Today, she was returning to work. A day earlier than recommended, but the call from Llewelyn an hour ago, ostensibly to see if she was enjoying her time off, carried an unspoken request to get her ass in to work ASAP.

Unrest still boiled in Maintenance. If her new task force was going to find the cause, she couldn't delay any longer. Rick and Amanda were back in the bullpen, and Sofie needed to pull herself together and join them.

She showered, dressed, and walked out to the street ten

minutes after getting out of bed. The bullpen was close enough that she didn't worry about fatigue, but far enough to test her ability to appear normal and rested to her partner — and her boss.

Something felt off about the atmosphere on the streets, like something big was coming. No protests, but too many people were hanging around. If the unrest was spilling into Authority, where Sofie lived, then the situation was already out of hand.

I should have checked the newsfeeds so I'd know what to expect.

The surgeon had told her to avoid screens. Her body was exhausted enough to keep her asleep most of the past three days, but now she felt detached from whatever was happening.

The sight of a stim-juice bar reminded her how much she missed the taste of blufroot. She'd had no stimulants at all during recovery. Now that she was able to stay awake long enough to eat and drink a glass of water, Sofie craved the jolt of energy.

She ordered three large, cold stim-juices, and grabbed a handful of flavor packs. "Any donuts? Or sweet buns?" she asked the clerk.

"Supplies are low," the boy said, pointing to the scanner for Sofie to pay. "We don't get so many in the morning as usual. What's there is what we got."

The pastry tray contained two dried out protein bars and a crumbly cookie. "I'll pass," Sofie said, tapping her credit chip.

At least she wasn't showing up on day one of the task force empty-handed.

.   .   .

THE BULLPEN WAS the first place that looked normal to Sofie after the ominous quiet of the streets. A few officers and detectives sat at desks, working or chatting. Rick stood behind Amanda looking at something on her screen. Both were serious.

"Morning," Sofie said. She placed the tray of drinks on Amanda's desk. "What's so interesting?"

"Trouble in Maintenance again," Amanda said. "We're going to have our hands full trying to figure out a solution."

Rick added an orange flavor pack to his drink. "You were completely offline. I can't imagine doing that."

"I needed rest," Sofie said. "I guess you partied?"

"Not all the time," he said. "I took a lot of naps."

Probably between partners, Sofie thought. "I'll let Llewelyn know we're ready to get started."

Amanda poked through the flavor packages and then took a drink of her plain juice. "He's been pacing."

"Yeah, I got the idea he was impatient from the tone of his call," Sofie said. "Did you get any rest?"

Amanda shrugged. She didn't normally share any personal information. "I got what I needed."

Sofie didn't even try to guess what she meant. Amanda might have spent the three days sucking up to the people who could give her a promotion, or partying in the Temporaries. As long as she was ready to work, it made no difference. She was probably more ready than Sofie.

"Did he say anything more about what we're supposed to be doing? As a task force?" Sofie needed a clear goal, not just 'figure out the problem and solve it' like in their last case.

Amanda shook her head and turned back to her screen.

Rick sat at his own desk. "I'd put money on him being as vague as possible. That way he can't be wrong."

"Or right," Sofie said. She sent Llewelyn a message requesting a meeting.

It didn't take more than ten seconds for him to pull open his door and bellow for the three of them to get in his office.

2

___

ofie stood by the door, worried that sitting and then standing again might trigger her vertigo. She would have to sit eventually, but not in the boss's office. She was so close to complete recovery, she couldn't take the chance something would go wrong. She'd been hiding her condition all her life. Her parents had kept it secret until she was capable of doing so herself. It would be stupid to get caught hiding it the minute she no longer had to worry about it.

"You all rested?" Llewelyn asked. "There won't be any days off for a while. And I'm guessing no nights, either."

"I'm good. The task force," Sofie said. "What are we investigating?"

Llewelyn leaned back in his chair and put his hands behind his head. The relaxed pose didn't fool Sofie. He was under pressure to do something, and it was going to be her job to get him results.

"The crime is tricky," Llewelyn said. He gave up on the pretend casualness and sat straight. "Someone is pushing the Maintenance and Manufacturing workers to violence. We kept a lid on it for the last couple of days. We can't keep it contained forever. That means we're going to lose control fast."

Sofie waited. Rick and Amanda stayed quiet too, probably to let any shit roll into Sofie's lap instead of their own.

"Okay. No one is dead, yet," Llewelyn continued. "We've got a few people in clinics because they've been assaulted. This kind of crime isn't one we usually get involved with, but the Intelligence squad haven't had any luck with it, so they dumped it on us."

So, something they'd usually assign to spies. "Why are they stalled?" Sofie asked.

"Not stalled," Llewelyn said. "The official word is they were brought in too late. They can't infiltrate now. They're better at the long game."

"So it's someone else's fault but they don't want to get caught saying it? And if everything goes off the rails, they want to be out of range of pointing fingers." She wasn't being given a choice, but Sofie didn't want her boss to think she was blind to the reality of the situation.

"Yes, but don't say that outside this office," Llewelyn said.

"Like Sofie asked, what's the crime?" Rick leaned on Llewelyn's desk as he spoke.

"Interference with commerce," Llewelyn said, "and probably some kind of treason against the Mallet. Meaning treason against the Elites. Your job is to find out who's behind all this and stop them."

Not an easy crime to solve.

"Someone is always interfering," Amanda said. "Which family is most pissed off?"

"All of them are," Llewelyn said. "I got the call about the

Intelligence squad just as you tied up your last case. Since then, no one has demanded we fix it. I can't get any Second to answer my calls. In the absence of pressure, I can only assume they are busy taking things into their own hands."

"The private security team?" Before Sofie's operation, they were only servicing the incoming temporaries. She'd noticed them helping a little with crowd control, but had they moved out to take over the entire station in the last three days?

"It's called Ulindia. An outfit with experience on a lot of planets, but nothing on a station. Not a great reputation if you're on the wrong side of them. They're still around, but only in the Temporaries. Both ends." Llewelyn rubbed his forehead in frustration. "Still apparently working for the Elites, but I'm not buying it."

"So we're supposed to be the heroes?" Amanda asked. "No other help?"

How can three detectives find a solution to a vague problem that Intelligence failed to even notice?

"I can't assign anyone to help," Llewelyn said. "You three have the highest solve rate, the widest set of skills, and a history of working well together. When the shit hits the fan, I'll have trouble stopping someone reassigning you to riot control if you're hanging around here."

Sofie shoved her hands in her pockets. Llewelyn was right. Rick was her partner, so she was glad to keep him on the team. She still didn't relish working with Amanda, but the woman had proven herself in the last case. Between them, they had contacts in every caste.

This was going to be a giant mess. The sooner they started the faster the case would be over. "Okay, so which room do we have?"

"None of ours," Llewelyn said. "I had a case room set up in Maintenance for you. People I trust to keep their mouths shut. The problem is in there anyway, so it makes sense for you to be close to the action."

He reached into a drawer to pull out three security passes, then slid them across the desk. They were blank gray plastic cards.

"You really trust the people who set up the room?" Sofie asked Llewelyn while taking her pass from Amanda.

"I paid them well and threatened them with retribution."

"Where exactly is the room?" Rick asked.

Llewelyn unfolded a piece of paper he'd taken from the drawer. "Here." He handed the address to Amanda. "Don't let anyone know what you're doing. Your contact is me for as long as I'm available."

"It's fully stocked?" Sofie asked. "Terminals, chargers, stim-juice machine?"

"Yes, Detective Allen, all the comforts of home." Llewelyn chuckled. "And you won't have to pretend to be working because I won't be there."

Like he really thinks we pretend.

"We should go," Sofie said. "I'll let you know if we need anything more than you supplied. Is there a specific contact in the families for us?"

"You have Nhu and Haadiya, and anyone you've formed a relationship with. Like I said, no one in the Elites is returning my calls. If that changes, I'll let you know."

Rick stood and glanced over his shoulder to the bullpen. "If we want to keep quiet, we should leave separately."

Amanda was the only one with the address.

"We can meet at that stim-juice bar," Sofie said, "the one in the next square."

"Get out of here and fix this," Llewelyn said as he turned away to read the screen above his desk.

"I want anything the Intelligence team found before they gave up," Sofie said.

"I'll ask, but don't wait for it."

3

S ofie watched Amanda and Rick leave the bullpen. They turned in opposite directions when they stepped out the door. It felt paranoid to take such precautions, but if anyone was watching and hoping to interfere, it would be worth the effort. The longer they could keep their location secret, the better chance they had of finding and stopping whoever was instigating the current trouble.

She'd never understood before why patients took so long to recover from operations, but being around people, even ones she knew well, was exhausting. She needed to be fully alert for this case. Lack of focus at any point, let alone a critical one, could end up destroying the Mallet. Right now, action was the only thing she could use to stave off the nap she wanted.

She counted to fifty and then left. The stim-juice bar was only a few minutes' walk, but she needed to take advantage of the time and check in with Bindes. He responded to her text with *call me*.

"You're already back at work?" he asked, instead of offering a greeting.

"No choice," she said. "I'm going undercover. What do I need to do to make sure I don't collapse or something?" Undercover was close enough to the truth that he would be able to give her usable advice. She wasn't ready to test his loyalty with the whole story yet.

"You shouldn't do it."

"Like I said, no choice."

He sighed deeply. "How are you feeling?"

"Tired."

"How long have you been at work?"

"Half an hour." Sofie stopped walking and stared into the window of a bistro to give her time to convince him. "It's just tiredness, no nausea, no vertigo."

"Okay. You need to get as much rest as possible. If you feel tired, take a break."

"What about some stimulants?" she asked.

"Not a chance. The operation was simple, but it's still brain surgery. I'm not giving you anything that will affect your hormonal balance."

That wouldn't be easy. She needed to be free of these restrictions. A lifetime worrying about the Fades hadn't prepared her for the few days she'd be terrified of dying from the cure. "How long is this going to last?"

"The next two days are critical," he said. "If you survive them, you'll be over it."

Two days. No guarantee the Mallet would stay quiet for that long. "Okay. If you don't hear from me, I'm fine."

"Or dead, right?" He ended the call before she had a chance to respond.

Rick stood beside a table on the street. He waved at her and held up a stim-juice cup as she approached.

"Where are we headed?" Sofie asked. "We can't risk being separated."

Amanda showed her the unit location and number. "Got it?" she asked. When Sofie nodded, Amanda dipped the paper in her stim-juice before tossing it into the recycler.

"Let's talk as we go," Sofie said. "We need to reach out for information. Have you tried Haadiya?" she asked Rick. "And maybe I can call Torque. He might know something we don't."

The unit was deep into Maintenance. The dark streets and the entrance to the Temporaries were close. She had no intention of sitting behind a locked door while Rick or Amanda did the real work on the streets. A quick trip to see Torque wouldn't count as exercise, and if she couldn't take a nap, moving around was the only way to stay awake.

"Haadiya hasn't called me back," Rick said. "Any luck with Nhu?"

Sofie shook her head. "Maybe they don't think it's important? Or maybe they have bigger problems."

"What about the protest leaders?" Amanda asked. "The ones in jail. Maybe they know something?"

Rick paused and tapped his pad. "Still in custody. We should get set up in the case room, figure out the supplies we'll need, and then go interview them."

A trip to the jail would be safe enough, Sofie thought. "Okay. We get the unit properly stocked and the equipment tested. We interview some people, and we figure out where to go from here?"

"The station is quiet right now," Amanda said. "We won't be able to move so freely if that changes."

AT THE UNIT, Sofie unlocked and rolled up the door. Leaving without being noticed would be hard if they had to do that every time.

Inside, the space was double the size of her quarters because it was two units. The connecting wall was gone, and Sofie noticed a door cut into the roll-up of the second unit.

The workspace was basic. A small kitchen unit in the second half, a bathroom in the first. Desks and monitors for five people.

Is Llewelyn sending more people?

One wall was covered in screens. Two showed the area immediately outside the units. The remaining four were constant feeds of the situation in the Mallet. The station looked peaceful for now.

"We'll need to get some premade meals," Amanda said. "Maybe a couple of cots. I don't think we'll be able to go home at the end of the day until we've solved this."

"Plenty of chargers," Rick said, pointing at a low shelf that ran the length of the second unit.

Three pad chargers and six stunner chargers were lined up on the first half of the shelf. Three sets of body armor were piled on the other end.

"Okay," Sofie said. "Looks like he did know what we needed. Let's get started."

Amanda hooked her pad up to one of the screens and the newsfeed disappeared. "Lots of room for notes," she said.

Sofie logged in to the official systems. "We've got high-level access now."

Amanda chuckled. "Good to know I won't have to use the hacked codes."

"Don't count on it," Rick said. "We might want to get some stuff without leaving a trail."

"Let's not get too comfortable," Sofie said. "I don't plan on us being here much. Put up all the names we think might help."

Amanda started typing and the screen filled with names. Not enough for Sofie to feel confident they would solve the case fast, but plenty to start with.

"Your doctor friend," Amanda said. "The one who works off the books, you think he'll know anything?"

"I'll be the contact there," Sofie said. "And Petra Starlight, the Support clinic doctor. She was good with data, maybe she'll see a trend in some medical records that will lead us to the perpetrator."

The four protest leaders' names went up next. Then Nhu, Haadiya, and the boss of the dark streets.

"You know who that is?" Sofie asked. Rick had told her he knew it was a man, but he'd never shared the name.

"No, but that doesn't mean we can't contact him," Amanda answered before Rick could.

"Set up the protest leader interviews, please, Rick," Sofie said. "We'll do them as a team."

4

The Mallet was almost thrumming with tension as Sofie led Rick and Amanda to the jail. In the time between entering their case room and leaving again, the people on the streets had changed from ignoring them to sending them small glances and muttered comments, and stepping to the side as though avoiding a contagious disease. It all added up to more than the usual dislike of cops.

When they crossed the threshold of the jail, a uniformed sergeant greeted them. "Your four perps are in conference alpha. You want them together or separate?"

Interviewing them separately gave Sofie a better chance of finding out something useful. If the protest leaders were together, they would go on the defense and Sofie wouldn't be able to pit them against each other.

"We need rooms. I want them alone waiting for us to call them in," she said. "Any idea who might be the weak point?"

The sergeant opened a scheduler on his pad. "I can give you interview seven, it's near the conference room. I don't have anyone to guard four rooms, so I can't separate them."

The man is doing his best. He shouldn't be this short on staff.

"Can you put someone in the room to keep them from talking to each other?" Rick asked. "When we've finished with each one, we can escort them back to their shared cell if it's a problem."

"No one goes to the cells except my people." He flicked something on his pad and then looked up. "I can give you one guy. You decide how to use him. Most of my staff are on riot control training. I gotta say, I don't know if any of them are up to it. We're mostly in our last years on the force."

"I'll watch the room," Amanda said. "I can work while I watch, and maybe I'll see something useful."

Sofie appreciated the offer. It left her with Rick for the interviews, and they'd worked out a system in all the years they'd been partners. "Okay. You can watch the feed. Between interviews, Rick can watch the room and you can give me your thoughts."

A few minutes later, Sofie sat across a table from a woman named Elsa Woo. Rick leaned against the wall, ready to be intimidating if she gave the signal.

"You organized the protests last week," Sofie said.

Elsa crossed her arms and sat back in the chair.

"No need to answer that," Sofie continued. "You didn't fight the charge, so we'll consider the answer a yes."

Still no reaction.

"We want the people who organized you," Sofie said. "They're getting away with everything, while you end up in a cell — or with a life sentence and find yourself in line to join the rest of the dead bodies in the composter." On the Mallet, a life sentence was death. No one was going to pay to keep prisoners alive for that long.

"You gonna ask a question?" Elsa asked. "I'm not stupid enough to start talking because you stop."

She's been here before. Thinks she's in control.

"Fair enough," Sofie said. "Who started this? Who told you to organize?"

"We started it because we'd had enough. Don't need nobody to organize us."

This was wasting time. Elsa enjoyed playing the tough hero of the masses. And if it was a power play, the best tactic was to shut her down and maybe come back to her later.

"Thanks," Sofie said. "Let's get you back in your cell."

Rick pushed off the wall and beckoned Elsa to follow him. She obeyed and didn't look back.

Outside, Rick handed Elsa off to the cop who would take her back to the cell block, and followed Sofie to the conference room.

"I hope we don't have to go through three more of those," he said. "We could be doing something more productive."

"Like what?" Sofie asked, blinking back exhaustion. "Yeah, I hate this kind of box-ticking work too, but you never know."

Amanda stepped aside to let Rick take over as babysitter. She joined Sofie in the hall, looking both ways to make sure they were alone.

"Anything?" she asked.

"Stubborn, and I'm pretty sure she didn't know what we wanted," Sofie said. "The others?"

"Not a word between them," she said. "Not that it mattered. Body language is hard to disguise for long."

Not for everyone, Sofie thought. I've been doing it for years, and anyone in the Executive could hide their feelings from an Elite. If they couldn't, they landed the shitty jobs.

"And?"

"So, Tom Sutter is scared. I don't know if he knows

anything, but he really doesn't want to be here. Gena Yellow-bird is relaxed. Maybe on some kind of sedative. I wouldn't trust anything you get from her."

"We'll still need to interview her," Sofie said.

"I think you need to take Lily Amir. She's got something to say and is eager to say it. I can't guarantee it's not just a lecture or a speech about human rights or something just as stupid, but she's ready."

"Okay, we'll take her next. If we get what we need, maybe we're done here."

"You still need to interview the others," Amanda said. "Unless you want to confirm she's the one who talked."

It was a good idea, Sofie thought. If she wasn't fighting sleep, Sofie would have thought of it herself. Amanda's words reminded her that this was going to be a hard case to solve. Not that the thought was far away. Usually, a culprit broke fast and then went to trial. These people, no matter how wrong-headed their actions, were trying to make the Mallet better for everyone who lived there.

"You should be in the room with me," Sofie said. "If she's ready to talk, we don't need Rick's looming threat. We need someone she'll see as reasonable."

Amanda smiled. "Thanks for the vote of confidence. Can I tell Rick?"

Sofie laughed and told her to bring Lily Amir to the interview room.

"First, I want to say I didn't want anyone hurt," Lily said as she sat down facing Sofie and Amanda.

"Okay," Sofie said. "What was the goal?"

She nudged Amanda's knee under the table to indicate she should take over.

"To show we are people," Lily said. "They treat us like products, or tools. That's not right."

"Why now?" Amanda said. "The upper castes haven't changed. So why was it suddenly so important to protest?"

"They said it was time," Lily answered. "The people who reached out. They said we shouldn't wait until it got worse."

A mysterious *they*. The same ones Anna Kivi feared enough to kill herself rather than face?

Sofie forced herself to let Amanda continue with the questioning. If she took over, it would go from a conversation to an interrogation, and that might shut Lily up. This early in the case, any lead was too valuable to screw up.

"Who reached out?" Amanda asked.

"I don't think anyone knows who did it. But they were right. I mean, that Sato Pratham was stealing kids. That woman was messing with the meds. What next? Anyone with a bit of power on the Mallet just uses it to beat us down."

How had the real information about Kivi and Sato gotten past the censors?

"How did they contact you?" Amanda asked.

"Messages," Lily said. "On my pad. Like the others. Just asking us how long before it was too late."

"Do you still have the messages?" Sofie asked.

"They told me to reset my pad. On the last day before you stopped us."

So, no way to trace the sender.

Sofie let Amanda finish the interview with a few more questions but Lily didn't know anything helpful. That, or Sofie didn't know enough to interpret any clues she let slip. Or she was too exhausted.

The interviews with Tom Sutter and Gena Yellowbird were fast and useless.

"I'll get their pads," Rick said. "Maybe one of them decided not to reset."

Sofie nodded. "We need to get back to the case room," she said. "I don't want to talk about it here."

5

In the case room, Sofie checked for messages while the others settled. The lead about the messages sent to the protest leaders, as weak as it was, had given her a much-needed boost of energy. "No news on any conspiracy," she said.

"I'm sure it won't be long," Amanda said. "Even as we explode, the media will find a way to stir up trouble rather than help calm the Mallet."

"So, we have something that feels like a lead but might be a dead end," Rick said. "You think we should ask for a trace on the deleted messages?"

Sofie had considered the question on the walk back to the room. "Maybe we need to find out if the same thing is happening with the people organizing the crowds now," she said. "If it's the same, we could track and intercept the new messages."

Llewelyn might be able to supply some names. If he could give them access to every database on the Mallet, it would help when they had a lead to follow. Being separated from the rest of the cops was disorienting. Or perhaps it was her recovery making her feel that way. She rarely used the support of her fellow officers in a case. This time she felt like she was struggling to see a path through to a lead. Or even assess whether a lead was useful or just a lie.

"We can ask," Amanda said. "It did sound like he wanted us to stay away, so maybe we need to have a list of requests before we reach out? Try to make this the last time."

"Let's put something on the screens first," Sofie said. "I'm not sure keeping this in our heads is going to work."

Amanda started typing while Rick made stim-juices for everyone.

Did Bindes mean me to avoid even the mild effect of a stim-juice? Do I care?

On the center screen words popped up, giving Sofie the distraction she needed to avoid thinking through the question.

SUSPECTS: none so far that she'd feel comfortable pointing to, but they had leads.

The four names of the protest leaders followed, along with a question.

Who is provoking the new problem?

Known facts: the leaders were contacted by message, the sender is not yet identified, the new leaders are unknown.

Questions:

Can we get blanket authorization for warrants?

Can we follow up with new sources?

Is there an undercover detail in the protest groups?

Who might benefit from violence?

AMANDA STOPPED TYPING.

"It's not much," she said. "I know it's early, but it feels like all we have is questions, and no idea who can answer them."

Sofie stared at the screen. Eventually more names would show up, and some would move to the culprit column. And more clues would rise out of the mess. But for now, Amanda was right. They needed to answer some questions. Even one answer would be progress.

"We can't let ourselves be stuck in here," she said. "No one is going to knock on the door and tell us everything we need."

"Okay," Rick said. "Where do you want to start?"

"If only I knew," Sofie answered. "But there is one question we can take a stab at. Who might benefit?"

"Someone who can get off the Mallet before the end," Amanda said. "Likely to be Elite or Executive."

"If this is coming from inside," Sofie said, "I'm having trouble understanding how an Elite benefits from slowing or stopping production. Or from the Mallet blowing up. I mean, that's the potential end result, right?"

"Or it's a customer," Rick said. "Someone trying for a better deal, or to get out of a contract?"

"They'd lose money on any product still waiting to be shipped," Sofie said. "Amanda, do you know if we can find out what each customer has here in the way of inventory? And if there isn't a lot, who cleared out first?" *Maybe it's so little they'd write the loss off.*

"Interesting idea. Yes, I can get my hands on the public records pretty easily. But we're back to asking for blanket access." Amanda started typing again. The words popped up on a second screen as she spoke. "I'll start a list of records and access we want. That way, if Llewelyn can't give us the highest level outright, we'll have a fallback position."

He said he'd get us whatever we needed, Sofie thought. But it didn't mean everything, just everything within his power.

"Anna Kivi said *they* were coming," Sofie said. "Maybe this is what she meant. If this is coming from off-station, we'll never stop it."

The list of places they'd need to access kept growing. Mostly databases for tracking everything. A blanket search warrant appeared as she watched. Then Amanda added the words, *all requests are to be kept confidential and refer to current and past transactions.*

"Next steps?" Sofie asked.

"Talk to Llewelyn," Rick said.

"Ask around. Our contacts might have something that helps," Amanda said. "If we can go to the captain with some concrete leads, he might be more helpful."

"Has anyone reached out yet?" Sofie asked. "Left a message? Asked for a meeting?"

Rick checked his pad. "Nope, and that's unusual. We can usually count on Haadiya showing up pretty early in important cases."

Nhu hadn't left a message either.

"None of my contacts responded to my calls," Amanda said. "Can we get any more isolated?"

This is way beyond our usual cases. I'm not sure the typical methods are going to help. It isn't a good sign that I feel like I'm just spinning my wheels.

"Is there any benefit to sharing our comms?" Sofie asked. "I mean, if I'm busy and Nhu reaches out, it would be better for one of us to answer, rather than hope they leave a message."

"I can set something up," Amanda said. "Let me know what you want to keep private."

Shit. How was she going to make sure nothing about her surgery or the Fades got up on a screen? Even if it was a mistake, her secret would be out. She needed to think about purging any communications with Bindes when they were done with this. "Not a top priority now. I think we should get some actions on the board and head out."

6

"Even if this is coming from off-Mallet," Rick said, "there has to be a high-placed contact here. Someone who might talk, with the right incentive."

"We'll need leverage to even talk to someone higher than Support," Sofie said. "Any ideas?"

No response, which was not a surprise.

"I guess it will be easier if we pick some actual people, rather than anyone in a high caste," she said. "Since Nhu and Haadiya have gone silent, it's up to us to figure out names."

Amanda started typing again. "All the liaisons," she said as names appeared on the screen. "Nine Elite families, I count twenty liaisons. You suspect any of your contacts being involved?"

Sofie didn't trust Nhu far, but if they were pushing for riots, she'd be shocked. "I think we can cross off the people we deal with. They'll eventually get back in communication, I hope."

Seven names disappeared. That meant Amanda had five

contacts at that level. No wonder she seemed to know so much.

"What are the family alliances?" Rick asked.

Amanda sorted the names into nine groups. "They're all represented."

"I know Haadiya is liaison to the Second, and Nhu to the Pratham. Do we have that information for the others?"

Amanda shuffled the names again. "You're thinking it will be harder to get to the Pratham liaisons?" she asked.

"I'm thinking the liaisons to the Seconds might have more secrets." Sofie nodded toward the screen. "The Seconds have wider reach than the Prathams because they oversee everything the family does. And we might find more leverage on the liaisons at that level. A Pratham will provide more cover for everyone who worked on their dirty business than a Second will."

"How do you want to split them?" Rick asked. "We've got six names."

It wasn't as easy as simply questioning the six people who worked with the Seconds. They needed to know more about the individuals, find something they could use for leverage. "We need authority to act," Sofie said. "And we need some information."

"And a plan," Amanda said. "It's not like we can bring them here for questioning. The station is too volatile for easy travel."

"Do you think you can find the leverage?" Sofie asked Amanda. "I'll contact Llewelyn about warrants and locations."

"I'll see what I can do," Amanda said. "I usually reach out to my contacts, but since they've all gone silent, it's me and the databases. My hacking skills are good, but they aren't great."

"What about me?" Rick asked.

"I wouldn't call your hacking abilities *skills*," Amanda said.

"Fair comment," Rick said. "But I'm not just muscle here."

"Let me talk to Llewelyn," Sofie said, ignoring the banter and pulling her pad off the charger.

He didn't pick up. She ended the call without leaving a message. "So much for him being there for us." Maybe their usual informants and help weren't going to be there for them either. That would make their job impossible. And, even more worrying, did Nhu and Haadiya carry the same power? If the Mallet was in turmoil, was it having an impact at the Elite and Executive levels?

"He does run the whole police department," Rick said. "Did you expect him to be sitting staring at his pad, waiting for your call?"

Sofie chuckled. Not completely right, but she did expect him to be there.

Her pad chimed. Llewelyn calling back. So maybe he was waiting for her to call.

"What do you want?" he asked before Sofie could speak.

"We need authorizations," she said.

"I can't talk about this on the open comms," Llewelyn said.

"We're on a secure line," Sofie said.

"Can't be trusted."

"Fine, I guess we'll come to you," Sofie said. "Are you in the office?"

"Where else? Be careful and be fast. Things are changing." He ended the call.

"So we go?" Rick asked.

Going in was wasting time, but there was nothing she

could do about it now. And if Llewelyn gave her what she asked for, they wouldn't need to go in much more before they had a result. It didn't mean she was willing to lose productive time for two people. "I'll go alone. You and Amanda figure out a plan. I'll be back as soon as I can."

7

Sofie checked the cameras before leaving the unit. The streets were clear; not exactly a normal situation for this time of day. Midday was not a shift change, which meant fewer people on the streets, but there should still be some. It meant no one would observe her when she left, though. It would take some time to feel comfortable moving about in the section as if it was normal for her, and it was important to blend in. Very few people without a shift on the line resided in Maintenance, and with the current atmosphere in the section, she didn't want to be seen as different.

The empty streets didn't continue far. Two intersections away, in the first square, a group of protesters with familiar orange and blue badges crowded into the center. No chants yet, but the grumbling was getting loud. She stepped to the side and walked slowly past, wanting to hear what they were complaining about, and at the same time, slip by unnoticed.

"It's not right."

"They should be freed."

"We want a voice, is all."

Not the same as before, and not cohesive, but it wouldn't take much to push these people to a protest — or a riot. Sofie glanced around looking for police, but none were in sight. Was that good or bad?

Capturing the leaders hadn't kept a lid on the unrest as everyone had hoped. If people were still protesting, it told Sofie more than what she'd learned from the interviews. They had less time than expected to find the person or persons responsible for stirring up the unrest. And new protest leaders had been waiting to step into the void.

Maybe Llewelyn knew the names of the instigators. If he could point them in the right direction, the case would be solved faster than trying to dig up leads when people were cut off from the main part of the station by protests.

She lingered at the entrance of the street leading to the bullpen to watch the crowd. It didn't look like the participants were escalating. Maybe she was wrong, and this was just a winding down of the original protests.

And maybe she was looking at the person who'd lead her to the source of the unrest. No one in this square looked like they had the power to take advantage of the chaos that would come. These were the victims, the people who'd be starving and abandoned if the Mallet failed. Not all of them, of course. At least one person in the crowd must be talking to whoever would benefit from the chaos.

She pulled out her pad and scanned the newsfeeds. Nothing about other crowds causing problems. Surely, the protests were still news, still something for the media to sell ads on.

She held up her pad and pretended to search for something on the network while she videoed the faces in the crowd. She made a mental note to ask Llewelyn for access to the drone feeds. Amanda would be able to work some magic and match faces to names.

When she finished, Sofie sent the video over a secure link to Amanda with a note.

She checked the faces of the people who weren't joining in. Some looked annoyed at the disturbance, but too many others looked like they wanted to walk into the crowd and start talking.

If there were still people in Maintenance who didn't want to upturn the current order, there was hope. It wouldn't last long. Joining a mob wasn't a rational decision, and sometimes letting off steam by breaking something felt too good to worry about the consequences.

Sofie tucked her pad away and turned to head for the bullpen. Her mind was tired, her body was fine. This was a new experience. Was it her recovery? Could she head home for a quick nap? Even as the thought came to her, Sofie shoved it back to the recesses of her mind. There was no time to nap. She needed stim-juice. And she needed to sort through her ideas. It was a worry that her brain wanted a rest so badly; she might not be thinking straight, and how would she know?

If she was getting muddled, it wouldn't take long for Rick, or Amanda for that matter, to notice. She was so close to being completely free of her condition, but this was the time when she needed to be more diligent, not to relax. Maybe she was anticipating the wrong thing. Did anyone on the Mallet relax completely? She needed to trust her ability to reason. Second guessing every decision would be worse than making wrong ones.

8

By the time she walked into the bullpen, Sofie felt the rush of stim-juice through her body. Her brain was alert, and she'd added more items to the list for Llewelyn. If he wanted them to work independently, he couldn't deny them the authority to do so. Unless the whole secrecy thing was to set them up for criminal abuse of power charges.

Paranoia. He wouldn't need to go through this much trouble if that was his plan.

Sofie greeted a couple of cops as she passed by on her way to Llewelyn's office. No one seemed suspicious of her absence, and no one seemed overly taxed with cases.

Llewelyn stood to greet her as she entered his office. "Let's get this done," he said. "Any updates?"

She sat and waited from him to set the privacy screening on the office. "I have a list of things we need," she said.

"Let's see it." Llewelyn held out his hand as if she was going to hand him a data film.

"It's in my head," she said. "First, there's something stirring again, did you know?"

"It's under control," Llewelyn said. "We've got eyes on the whole section. No one is getting beyond a grumble. My contacts in the media don't have any news either."

So he must know about the crowd she'd witnessed. "We need access to the drone feeds," she said.

"I can give you the police ones," he said as he typed something into his pad. "You think you can find a contact in the media for theirs? And those Ulindia assholes have drones out too."

Would more data be a distraction? "Just ours for now," she said. "We have surveillance everywhere, right?"

He nodded. "What else?"

"We need authority," she said, testing out his boundaries.

"For what?"

The question didn't help her figure out if he had a line he wouldn't cross. "Warrants for records, for searching locations, for arresting people we can't name yet."

He sat back in his chair and clasped his hands over his gut. He didn't answer right away, and Sofie found herself thinking up excuses before he told her no.

"That's a lot of power," he eventually said. "We have rules to stop people doing whatever they want without oversight for very good reasons."

People with unlimited power never seemed to use it to make life better for anyone. Not just on the Mallet. But this wasn't normal times. And Sofie wasn't asking for sole power.

"Between the three of us, I think we can restrain our world domination urges," she said. "Do you want us to stop this problem before it hits critical mass? We can't wait around for authority to act every time we get a lead."

"Give me five minutes," he said. "Alone."

Sofie stood and waited for Llewelyn to release the security on the door.

Five minutes. Thinking, or asking for permission? No matter, she had the drone feeds. They needed a location for interviews. Would it make sense to do that here? Get a room set aside for their use only. Have it converted for interrogation. She sat in the administrative assistant's empty desk. He must be running errands, because normally, Llewelyn had him guarding access to the office.

Right now, the team could walk around the Mallet freely. So bringing people here for questioning made sense. Doing it in a jail setting would leave a trail, and it came with rules. Not that she intended to do anything illegal to a subject, but threats often came in handy. And if it meant saving the lives of everyone on the Mallet, maybe she would be willing to step into the darker side of that gray area.

Llewelyn's voice came over the intercom on the desk. "Get back in here."

Sofie stood and pushed at the door. It didn't move. Then she heard a click as the lock disengaged.

"I can't give you carte blanche," he said. "My contact isn't available right now to issue the order. How long before you need it?"

"ASAP," Sofie said. "We don't have anything right now, but I still have items on my list for you. One of them might result in us needing to bring people in for questioning."

"What items?"

"A place to interrogate people."

"And? Give me everything, Sofie."

He didn't usually call her by her first name. Was it an attempt to put her off her guard?

"We need the names of the people instigating the new

unrest." There were probably a hundred other things if she had time to think it all the way through, but it was a start.

"If you want to question one of these people, you can't keep coming here," he said. "Try to avoid going to the same places all the time. Don't go home the same way every time. In fact, if you can avoid it, don't go home at all."

"You think we're being watched?"

"If not yet, then soon. Ulindia is making noise about offering assistance in the emergency, like we'd welcome a private security company's help. The problem is we might not have a choice. This escalates, and the people driving the protests take hostages? We don't have enough people to do everything."

"That room we have isn't big enough to hold a prisoner or interrogate anyone." Sofie thought while she spoke. "I'm not complaining, but we need a space nearby, maybe next door, to use for holding people. And we need that blanket authority. If you're right, we won't be able to come for permission every time we need to act."

"I'll keep working on it. In the meantime, I'll find a list of nearby empty units. You can use your police override to access them. And I'll send along the names of anyone we know who might be provoking the masses."

It was a start. "If we need more —" Sofie waved her hand like she was erasing the words. "No. *When* we need more, how do we get in touch?"

"Send a message here." He handed her a contact card. "It's high security, and I'll check it every thirty minutes. I'll get back to you as fast as I can."

Sofie took the card and stuffed it in a pocket. She sent a message to Rick and Amanda to clear out their own units and meet back at the case room in two hours. Time to go get her clothes and spend her last moments at home for a while. She could set a timer for a short nap, and she needed to prepare to settle in the case room for the duration.

er partners were waiting at the same stim-juice stand as earlier. Rick was holding a tray of juice and a bag with grease stains on the side. Like Sofie, they each carried packs of belongings, and no one was overburdened. Amanda wore a long coat that hung too heavy for the material it was made of. Weapons? Tech? Sofie didn't want to ask in public.

"Ready?" she asked, taking a stim-juice from Rick.

"I did a search on the names we got from Llewelyn," Amanda said, "and the units we can use."

"Let's talk about it in private," Sofie said. "We don't want anyone taking interest before we're ready to act."

Rick put the bag on the table and then shifted his pack on his shoulders. "I picked up some extra premades just in case. We should probably do an inventory as soon as we get in the unit."

Sofie's pack contained medical supplies. Not enough to deal with major injuries, but there were stims and restoratives as well as bandages, blood clotting powder, and sanitizers. "Okay," she said before turning toward their new home.

While they walked, Sofie scanned the streets. Her usual shortcuts and hiding places were still available. If the authorities started erecting blockades, that would change. And if Ulindia had decided to help regardless of Llewelyn's preference, they weren't showing their faces yet. A few drones floated ahead of their group, not paying attention to anything particular. They were media and police surveillance, nothing unusual. The people around them were headed towards the next square, not in the direction of any workstation, and that worried her.

"Hear that?" Rick asked a moment later.

It was impossible to miss. Ahead in the next square, someone was stirring up trouble. The chanting was back, and this time it had a hard edge. They were too far away to catch the words. But that square was the most direct route to their case room.

Sofie pulled Rick and Amanda to a stop. "Wait."

"We can go the long way," Amanda said. "We'll find out what happened from the newsfeeds."

"Yes, we'll do that, but we can't miss this opportunity," Sofie said.

"If it kicks off, our packs will get taken," Rick said. "And Amanda's coat. We don't want anyone getting their hands on what's in there."

"You two go the long way," Sofie said. "I'll check out what's happening. If I can't find a way through, I'll back out and follow you."

"Not a chance," Rick said.

"I'll come with you," Amanda said. When both Sofie and Rick started to argue, she held up a hand until they stopped. "Sofie can't go alone. Rick, you are more likely to attract the attention we don't want. Two women can slip through faster.

We're no threat. We'll look like residents who don't want to get involved. You look like a cop."

Rick looked to Sofie for backup. She looked at the ground to think, then shook her head. "She's right. You take our packs and her coat. We'll wear earpieces, and if anyone gets in trouble, we call for help."

"I don't like it," Rick said.

"You don't have to like it," Amanda said. She shrugged off her pack and handed it to him. "The contents of my coat are in the lining."

She took it off, folded it carefully lengthwise, and hung it on Rick's outstretched arm.

Sofie removed her earpiece and contact card from a pocket in her pack and passed it to Rick. He looked like a delivery man festooned with unwrapped packages — well, like a delivery man who used to be a cop.

"Comms check," Rick said.

"One," Sofie said.

"Two," Amanda said.

"Three," Rick said. "Okay, it's working. Don't hang around. I'll have treats for you when you arrive." He held out the greasy bag, which he'd managed to keep hold of despite his load of belongings.

They watched him leave and then Amanda led the way forward.

The noise was coming from about twenty people in the center of the square. The chants were different this time. Not about life being unfair. Calls to action.

Stop the Elites. Hold fast. Fight for family.

More worrying than the new demands were the potential weapons. Sofie nudged Amanda and tipped her head to the edge of the crowd. Holo placards were replaced with physical ones. Metal bars, probably stolen from a store unit. Plastic signs attached, painted blue with the word *ENOUGH* in orange.

Amanda touched Sofie's elbow and guided her to the closed storefronts. "We need to move," she whispered.

Sofie took one look up to check that the drones were capturing the scene, regretting leaving her pad with Rick. Three official black drones, two from the most prominent media outlets. As she watched, six gray drones entered the square.

"Come on," Amanda whispered again, this time with a tug on Sofie's arm. "Something bad is about to happen. We can watch from the other side where we can run if we need to."

When they were safely on the street watching the action, Sofie pointed out the new drones. "Ulindia?"

"It was only a matter of time," Amanda said. "Let Llewelyn deal with it."

Sofie turned her attention back to the crowd. Amanda's prediction came true. Two people started shouting back at the crowd. The people with placards stepped forward as one. Another resident joined the fight, protecting the two who wanted it to end. Then another, and suddenly violence boiled over.

Placards became spears. The counter-protesters grabbed stools from the sidewalk, others joined in with knives held out.

Amanda pulled Sofie backwards.

"One second," Sofie said, resisting her. "Listen."

Boots stamping on the metal floors. Lots of boots, coming from the streets on the far side of the square. The brawlers stopped for a breath and then, as if wanting to do as much damage as possible before the cops arrived, they started the fight again. People went down, blood blooming.

Sofie turned and ran, Amanda beside her.

10

Rick waited for them in their room, and the door popped open as Sofie reached for the access pad. Amanda followed her through, and they both stood bent over, panting until they caught their breath.

"I haven't run that fast, ever," Sofie said. "We'll be inside for a while. The riot will be under control by now, but someone will be watching for any suspicious activity." And anything out of the ordinary would be suspicious for the next couple of hours.

Rick piled their packs in a corner and hung Amanda's coat from a hook on the wall.

"We'll be fine," Rick said. "I got into the drones so we can see when it's clear. Maybe with some work, we can commandeer a couple to float where we want them to, rather than hope to find one at the action."

"Anything from Llewelyn?" Amanda asked. "Other than the drone codes?"

"You don't believe I could have hacked them?" Rick asked, feigning hurt.

"Since no one is banging on the door to arrest you, no,"

Amanda said. "We got the codes for this an hour ago. Did you think the message was only for you? Check your pads. He said the names will take a few more hours. Although maybe we'll get lucky with the latest arrests. And I've got a list of units we can use for questioning."

So, Llewelyn had told the truth about trying to help. They couldn't rely on him every time if it took this long to access a list of names. "I guess we don't have authority," Sofie said. She pulled her pad from the pack on the floor and checked Llewelyn's messages. "He didn't even mention it."

"It's a good thing we don't have a hot lead," Amanda said. "If we have to stay in here, we should get started."

She tapped her pad and a screen lit up on the wall. A map with their location in red and three other units highlighted in blue.

"We'll scope them out as soon as it's safe," Sofie said. "Let's unpack and see what we've got."

Ten minutes later their belongings were laid out on the long shelf and their clothing hung on hooks.

"A small arsenal," Sofie said. "We should be fine as long as we can keep them charged, and we don't end up in a fight with someone who has more than a stolen metal bar to use."

"The medical supplies were a good idea." Rick picked up the packs and read the labels. "But if someone gets seriously hurt, we'll need a doctor."

Bindes would fill that role. He might even make a unit call if Sofie begged. "Let's try to keep any injuries within the scope of what our supplies can heal."

The food stacked against the far wall would keep them going for about a week. Sofie had no hope that they'd survive that long if the case wasn't solved fast.

"We need contacts," Rick said. "Eyes on the street. If it's

just us, we'll be stuck in here every time it gets crazy out there."

They needed a lot of things. Sofie didn't usually solve cases by sitting at a desk, but the cases she'd solved in the past were never about plots to destroy the Mallet. "Are you willing to share names?" The question was for Rick and Amanda. Sofie would add her contacts to the list, of course. But her contacts were not people likely to be out in a riot.

"I don't think we have any choice," Amanda said. "I'll start a list and then we can agree on what we want from them."

Sofie put up the three names she thought would be helpful. Dr. Bindes, Torque, and Petra. No one needed to know the details about Bindes' involvement in her life.

Rick added names, each coming with a short comment on the relationship — mostly lovers.

Amanda added names without any further detail. When they were done, they had seventeen possible spies.

"Let's call them," Sofie said. "Find out if they're willing to help. I don't want anyone on the team who'll feed us bullshit just to look important. Then we ask for information."

They separated as much as the small space allowed to reach out. Sofie pulled up Bindes's contact information, but before she could hit call, her pad chimed with an unknown contact.

"Yes?"

"You know who I am?" The voice was male. Sofie didn't recognize it. The words came out distorted; he was using a manipulator.

"No. And I don't have time for games. Who are you?"

"Well, honesty is refreshing," the voice said. "I'm glad the disguise is working. I'm the boss of the dark streets."

It must be a joke.

"Why would I believe you?"

"I protected you several times in my neighborhood. I let you search for that Pratham's murder site. Oh, and I punished the man who attacked you, by the way."

Someone might have guessed at some of those events, but the assault? No one knew the details. Sofie tried to think why anyone would impersonate the boss of the dark streets. No reason was good enough to make the eventual punishment worth it.

"Say I believe you," she said. "Why are you calling?"

"It is me, but I understand your suspicion," the man said. "The situation on the Mallet has been allowed to deteriorate too far. The people in charge are ignoring the problems. I don't make credits if people are rioting."

"You have some information to help us?" If the boss of the dark streets knew who was inciting the violence...

"Nothing yet," he said. "I will contact you if I hear something useful. This call is to get my number in your pad. If you need anything, reach out to me."

The call ended. Neither Rick nor Amanda was paying attention. They were talking to their contacts. Rick said he knew the boss of the dark streets was a man. He'd denied knowing more, but was he lying about that?

When Rick ended his call, Sofie asked him again if he knew the boss's identity.

"I don't know who it is," Rick said. "I got told it was a man by someone I trust."

Amanda ended her call and Sofie told them who reached out.

"I guess I can add him to the list of contacts," Amanda said. "I don't like what goes on in there, but he'll have people who can walk the streets and tell us what we need to know."

11

"We need to talk about this," Sofie said. Accepting the offer without any thought was an act of desperation. They badly needed a lead, and now one of the worst people on the Mallet offered help.

"You mean, what do we ask him to look for?" Rick asked.

"No," Sofie said. "He's got an ulterior motive. We can't just blindly walk into an agreement with him."

"Whatever he wants, we can find a way to avoid the worst when the riots are over." Rick looked to Amanda. "You agree, right?"

"No." Amanda added the boss to the list of possible leads. "Reneging on a deal with someone like that is stupid."

"We should call Llewelyn," Sofie said. "At least let him know we've got an offer of help. He can cover our asses later."

Sofie needed them to agree. As the leader of the task force, she could tell them what to do. They couldn't be a democracy, those eventually broke down, but she wasn't going to be an autocratic leader. This was the first major decision on the case, and her opportunity to create the atmosphere she wanted: one of collaboration. Then, if it came to one person deciding, maybe the others wouldn't feel like they were being ordered around. It was vital because Sofie didn't plan on being stuck where she could make decisions on demand and miss out on the action, and the team needed to be cohesive.

"I don't think you should call Llewelyn," Amanda said. "What if he says no? Or tells us to set a trap?"

Calling the captain was a bad idea for those reasons and for the precedent it set. He expected them to run without oversight. He trusted her to solve a problem without creating fifty more.

"It would help to know who it is," Sofie said. "I feel like trusting him is going to be one of those choices that looks really stupid in hindsight."

"I don't think that would help," Rick said. "Someone like that, he's covered his tracks. It would make a difference if it was someone we knew. But getting a name won't lead anywhere. He called you, so you must have a history with him."

A recent and troubling one. The boss of the dark streets had provided safe passage and warnings over the last month. Before that he'd been just another faceless criminal. "We need his people," she said finally. "No matter what happens, he's still stuck here on the Mallet with us. I have a feeling he can't leave. Maybe only because he would have by now."

"He commands loyalty from his people," Amanda said. "If they trust him, maybe we can take the chance."

That loyalty came at a price, and Sofie was sure that if any of the residents of the dark streets got a better offer, they'd switch sides in a blink.

"We can't just waffle about this," Rick said. "We can ask for his help and tell him we want to know the cost before we take it. That way we go in knowing what we'll be asked to do later. As I see it, he's no different from any of the Elites. They all want payment for anything they give. Just because he provides a safe place for the desperate doesn't mean he's any worse."

We all want his help. Why am I so reluctant?

"I think we'll end up regretting it," Sofie said. "I'll do what Rick suggested unless you have a better idea, Amanda."

"Ask me that when this is done," she said, chuckling. "This isn't the last time we'll have to put our misgivings aside and partner with a shady character."

I hope not.

"We can't have this discussion every time," Sofie said. "I'll ask the boss to find out who the leaders of the riots are. I'm not going into the dark streets this time, so if he doesn't tell me what he wants in return for the information, I can cut off any negotiation."

"So in the future?" Rick asked. "If some other criminal wants to help? What do we do?"

"We want the Mallet to survive, right?" Sofie asked. "We don't want life here to be worse than it was, but saving the station is the primary goal."

"I'm not sure there's anyone with the power to make it worse," Amanda said. "So we weigh the value of their help?"

"Yes, and no one makes alliances alone," Rick said.

Planning how to proceed in a case that was still a black hole felt like false progress, but their relationship as a team would be stronger for it.

"Okay, so we're keeping Llewelyn in the dark as well?" Amanda asked.

That felt like a step too far for Sofie. Only the fact that she trusted Rick and Amanda not to take them down a bad road made her agree. "We only contact him for help if we can't get it any other way."

Sofie took a moment to clear her thoughts. Contacting the boss of the dark streets when your mind was busy trying to save the world was a bad idea. Even though he'd offered to help, she knew it wasn't out of civic duty. She pressed the contact and waited for him to answer. When he did, she told him what they needed.

"Should be fast," he said.

"What do you want in exchange?"

"I saved your ass more than once without taking payment," he said.

"What is this going to cost us?" She would not engage with him in discussing the past.

"Anonymity."

"I have no idea who you are," she said.

"That might change. I want the Mallet to continue, most of us do. When it's over I might want to shed my past. Guarantee me that no one will find out who I am."

The price could have been higher. "If I am the only one who knows, I guarantee my silence. I can't speak for my team."

"You will encourage them to agree," he said. "I will do what it takes to get their guarantees."

12

S ofie passed on the boss's response. "I guess we wait. Should we check out the other units?"

Using empty units for interrogation and jailing was a good option. Each would have amenities, and without a code, no one would be able to leave. Unless the Mallet failed, at which point all doors would open to allow the thousands of inhabitants to fight over the hundreds of escape pods. Pods that might not have been maintained. Sofie wouldn't be concerned about prisoners if it came to that.

"What about getting the authority?" Amanda asked. "Didn't Llewelyn say he'd get back to us?"

"If we don't get it, we'll just have to do what it takes and cover it up later," Rick said.

They'd done that in the Sato murder case. Sofie thought at the time it was the right thing. The person they pinned it on was dead, and far from innocent. She'd said it wasn't the first step down a dark path, but maybe it had been for Rick. One cover-up for justice, the next for expedience, the next for credits?

"Good thing we don't have any leads," she said. "Llewelyn will call. I'm sure of it."

"We can keep reaching out to our contacts," Amanda said. "Maybe we won't need the boss of the dark streets."

Calling people would give them an idea of the situation across the station. The newsfeeds were repeating the images of the riot and nothing else. If the Support and Authority sections still didn't know how bad things were, they needed to be told. If riots were breaking out elsewhere and the coverage was suppressed, Sofie's team needed to know.

"I fucking hate being stuck here," Sofie said. "Go ahead and reach out."

Her pad chimed before any of them could act. Llewelyn calling.

She answered and put the call on speaker.

"I'm sending you a new team member," Llewelyn said. "Nhu Eckerman. They'll give you the warrants and authority you need."

Having an Executive in the room with them was going to be more of a hindrance than a help. Sure, Nhu would have some ability to clear the way for arrests and searches, but being mindful of their status and showing the proper respect when tossing out ideas was not going to be easy.

"Is there some way we can just keep open contact with them without bringing them here?" Sofie asked. "I mean, an Executive's safety is more important than most things, and they will be safer in their own section."

"I don't have time to argue with you, Allen. Nhu is on the way. They know the situation and are ready to stay inside the unit."

Sofie hadn't even thought about living with Nhu. "The quarters are basic," she reminded him. "Are they prepared to sleep on the floor?"

"Look, I've got thirty people to process here from that riot. And I need to prepare for a lot more unless you figure out how to end the violence. Let us get on with our job and maybe I'll get you some names to investigate. Eckerman is aware of the situation." He ended the call, leaving Sofie staring at the dark screen of her pad.

"Fuck," Rick said. "Just so you know, I plan to spend as much time as possible outside the unit."

"If Nhu decides it's too dangerous for them to be here, we'll be stuck escorting them back to Executive." Amanda started typing rapidly on her pad. "We can't leave anything out for them to see. Only what we know to be true."

Sofie put her pad on the charger and then sat at a desk. Llewelyn would never have agreed to this if he thought there was a chance Nhu's presence would hinder them. "Hang on," she said. "We have a bit of time. I'm sure they aren't going to knock on the door in the next few minutes. Llewelyn would know we need time to prepare."

Amanda shut down the screens and then looked at Sofie. "You need to set the rules right away," she said. "If Nhu is here to help, they should be willing to drop all formalities and agree not to use anything they hear or see in the unit against us."

Paranoia was new for Amanda. Having an Executive observe her work should be a good thing in her eyes. She knew better than Sofie how to handle difficult political situations. If Amanda was worried, there was good reason.

Sofie nodded and gestured to Rick. "You can't hide from this. We need to get out, yes, but having a command center is vital to our success. Amanda's right. I will respectfully set the rules when Nhu arrives. We have to make an effort too, right?"

Rick's use of charm and flirting as a social lubricant

wouldn't go down well with Nhu. They didn't seem to notice or care about him in that way — or anyone else.

"Fine. What if they don't agree to the rules?" he asked.

"Then we use one of the empty units to do the real work," Sofie said. "To be totally honest, I'm more worried that Nhu will have to keep asking someone in the Elite for the permissions we need. Unless someone at the top has delegated all authority to them, Nhu won't be much help."

13

_____

"Eckerman is here," Rick said, nodding toward the door camera display.

Sofie opened the door and beckoned Nhu in. Today they were dressed in gender neutral gray slacks, shoes, and a form-fitting sweater. They handed Sofie a matching gray pack and walked to the center of the room to survey the walls.

Sofie tossed the pack into a corner. Nhu could sort it out later. Best to set expectations fast; no one was a servant here.

"You have good coverage," Nhu said. "I may add a few items, but this will do. Where do we sleep?"

Sofie contained her response because rolling her eyes was likely to get her into trouble. The _we_ could be for the team, or for Nhu alone. It didn't matter; the answer was the same. "The floor, although we haven't slept here yet. And we don't have much time before the station is lost to the riots, so probably no sleep anyway."

"That will not suffice." Nhu pulled their pad from a pocket and flicked the screen awake. "I'll have the unit next door converted to quarters fit for us."

Sofie reached to stop Nhu going any further. "This location is secret, Nhu."

They glanced at her and kept typing. "The work will not reveal our location. The official reason is to accommodate the police should violence break out."

"Again," Amanda said, "violence has already happened."

Sofie waited for Nhu's reaction. People didn't contradict Executives. Nhu stood still for a long moment, then something happened and their face relaxed.

"Yes, I am aware of that. However, the lie will still accomplish our goal. If we are not able to rest, we will make mistakes. This team is the only one able to save the station now."

"When is the work being done?" Sofie asked. If it couldn't be stopped, she wanted it to be completed before the next riot.

"Within the hour," Nhu said. "The family is being relocated as we speak. The unit will be sanitized, and extra bunks added to the wall. They will loosen one of the connecting panels to speed up any further orders. When I receive confirmation that it is done, I will remove the unit from the logs."

Maybe Nhu is a good addition to the team.

"You have tools to remove the panel from this side?" Nhu asked.

"Not yet," Rick said. "Maybe the workers can leave a hammer and a drill in the unit?"

Nhu looked at the cameras. Sofie followed their gaze. Three Maintenance workers placed tool kits on the floor in front of the next unit.

"Good idea," Sofie said. She needed to take back control of the team before Nhu became too comfortable giving orders. "While we wait, I'd like to understand the level of authority you have, Nhu."

"Everything," they said. "Whatever you might need to move forward in the case, I will approve."

That wasn't normal. The only people on the Mallet with that level of power were the Elite families. That much power could only be delegated to an Executive by a Pratham.

"Nhu, we can give you a situation report, but first, I need to know we are working together as a team," Sofie said carefully. "No castes in here."

She tensed, trying to think of ways to circumvent Nhu if they didn't agree. Rick and Amanda kept their gazes on the screens, avoiding being drawn in. Sofie knew they were on her side, but this conflict, if there was one, was between her and Nhu. As long as she'd worked with them, she still didn't know what to expect.

Nhu finally nodded. "I agree. We all have valuable skills. I see you have taken the lead, Sofie. I will defer to you as the leader. Just one condition."

Always a price.

"What do you want?"

Nhu smiled, an expression Sofie had rarely seen them wear. "Patience. My whole life I have been pandered to, and I suspect I will not change quickly."

"Agreed," Sofie said, relieved. "We'll all need to get used to it. So, how did you get the power to authorize anything we need?"

"The Elite are gone." Nhu said the words without intonation.

Everything went quiet. The faint noises in the next unit faded, and the air felt thick. Sofie glanced at her team members. Rick's face was white. Amanda just stared at Nhu.

"They left us here to die?" Amanda asked. "They think the station is going to fail?"

Nhu took a seat and seemed to collapse now that the news was out.

"Who else knows this?" Sofie asked.

"Just the liaisons, and you," Nhu said. "My colleagues are well aware of the consequences of this becoming public knowledge."

"We'd never be able to stop it," Rick said. "If the rioters find out the Elites are gone, we won't be able to contain the violence."

"So my peers will keep their secret for now. I assume they are seeking ways to leave, but there are no ships available." Nhu nodded to the media screen. "You need to act fast. No, *we* need to act fast."

If the media even suspected the Elite families were gone... what could they do? No point in sensationalizing the headline. Anyone left on the Mallet would be dead. Either fast in a riot, or slowly as the Mallet's life support systems failed.

14

The Elites were gone. Sofie couldn't make sense of it. "What about the clients?" Sofie asked. "I mean, work continues regardless of the pockets of violence. Who are the clients talking to? What about the incoming ore and supplies?"

"All questions to be answered when we have stability," Nhu said. "I came here as soon as I learned of the evacuation. No one told me or any of my colleagues that they were going. We all found out when we realized our respective Elites were not here to answer questions or give orders."

"They abandoned you?" Rick asked.

"It seems they did just that."

"All the liaisons?" Amanda asked. "Wherever they went, the Elites will need someone to do your jobs."

"Not all. A few liaisons appear to be missing. I cannot be sure whether they were taken along, or disposed of," Nhu said. "This discussion is not productive."

Sofie wondered how Nhu could be so casual about such a fundamental change. "I'm sorry, Nhu. No one is arguing that we don't need to move forward, but this is important. If the Elites knew this was coming, or ignited the riots, we have a very different job to do."

They sat straighter and seemed to look up at Sofie while still looking down on her. "I understand the problem, Sofie. I don't see the point of worrying about something we can't possibly know."

Rick pushed away from the wall and joined Sofie. "Do you think the Elites are going to come back?"

Nhu frowned as if they hadn't even considered the question before. "We searched the residences and nothing of importance was left behind. Perhaps they will return, perhaps not. I may have been the Ruiz liaison, but I was never able to understand how their minds worked. Yes, everything orbited around power and money — power, mostly — but like you I cannot fathom a reason for them to leave."

Sofie closed her eyes, hoping to shift her whirling thoughts from the fact that they had no leadership to a plan for moving forward to solve the crisis. No one but the remaining liaisons knew. That wouldn't last long. "If the Elites plan to cause the Mallet to fail — I still can't believe it — they only have to reveal their absence. We need to know why they haven't done that." She opened her eyes to see Nhu smiling again.

"A very good insight, Sofie. Perhaps that is where I can bring value to the team. I have some understanding of the contracts with the corporations we provide services to, and the founding contract. The agreement between the Elites and the people of the Mallet from the last upheaval."

"What agreement?" Amanda asked.

"When the Elites took power, they signed a charter of sorts," Nhu said. "The educators were ordered to purge it from the history lessons."

"This charter might explain their leaving?" Rick asked.

Nhu gave an elegant shrug and reached for their pad. "Or provide us with a way to substitute another leader."

"Do you need help?" Sofie asked. "You were right. We need to get back to our initial goal. We should have some names soon. We need to talk to our own contacts, ask for help, or at least make sure they're safe."

"I will ask if I need assistance," Nhu said, flicking their pad on. "I do not believe anyone has enough knowledge to help. But you have your own tasks."

"You said some of the liaisons are also gone." Rick cleared his throat. "Haadiya? Is he still on the station?"

Nhu looked up from their pad. "He is. I believe he has gone to a hiding place. Somewhere to wait out the crisis. You will be reaching out, I assume?"

Rick nodded and pulled his pad off the charger.

Sofie sat and looked at the screen where they'd listed their contacts earlier. One name would be easy to call. "Llewelyn," she said. "We need to go to him."

"He said we were on our own," Amanda said. "He's dealing with problems arising from us not solving the case."

A particularly bitchy way to put things, Sofie thought. "I need to see him, give him an update."

Nhu frowned at her. "Do not tell him about the Elites."

"I won't, but you can be sure he'll figure it out pretty fast when they aren't pestering him for results." She looked at the newsfeeds. "This might be our last chance to go to the bullpen. Llewelyn might have answers. And we need a channel to reach him in emergencies."

Amanda closed her pad screen and tucked the device into her pocket. "I agree. The streets are quiet right now. We can reach out to our contacts from the bullpen as easily as here. And I don't like feeling as if we've been set up to take a fall. We need something concrete to use if someone thinks we've overstepped. Coming, Rick?"

Rick stood. "I can't get Haadiya to answer. Let's go. Nhu, you'll be safe here."

Nhu waved him away and kept reading.

15

The streets were eerie. No people. Business doors rolled down. Silence.

"Hang on," Sofie said, stopping and checking the area for hiding places.

"I don't think this is a good sign," Rick said. "It feels like everyone is gone. Like the station was evacuated while we sat talking."

No one could evacuate the Mallet that fast. Even if they tried, there was only enough transportation for a small percentage of the population.

"Can you scan the drones from here?" she asked Amanda.

"No, and the feeds are down too." Amanda pointed to the black screens in each corner of the square. "You want to go back?"

The last thing Sofie wanted to do was run and hide. The problem wouldn't be solved sitting inside, trawling through data. "We can't give up without knowing why people are staying away. Maybe the feeds are only cut off here. Give me a second."

She tapped her pad and Nhu's face appeared. "Yes?" they said.

Sofie asked about the newsfeeds.

"The screens here are showing normal," Nhu said. "No blank areas."

"Can you see this square?" If the screens were showing Maintenance as normal, someone with a lot of power was controlling the Mallet. And the Elites were gone so she had no clue who it could be.

"I see nothing at your location. Not even you."

"The screens are down here, and I don't see one drone. Give us a minute."

Sofie beckoned Amanda and Rick closer. There was no need for them to keep watching an empty square. "Check to see if someone tampered with the screens," she said.

"Sofie," Nhu said, their voice quiet.

"We're checking for sabotage."

"Someone is feeding a loop on your location. I have no idea if that's true for the entire Mallet."

If every screen on the station was playing recorded images, something truly bad was going on.

"We need to know," she whispered back.

"I'm tagging your location. When you move, I can check the screens."

"The cables have been cut," Amanda said.

So whoever is urging the residents to violence is capable of more than just manipulating angry people.

Sofie relayed the information to Nhu.

"Can you split up?" Nhu asked. "I can tag all three of you. It will be the fastest way to learn the extent of the interference."

Every instinct screamed at Sofie to stay together. Her rational mind agreed with Nhu. It was more important to know if the entire station was out of touch with reality than to get confirmation from Llewelyn.

"We can't cover the entire station," she said. "I'll continue on this route. Rick can head for the Support section through the shortcuts. Amanda can circle around Maintenance, so we have more than this path to the bullpen covered."

"We meet back at the bullpen?" Rick asked.

Amanda pressed her lips together, thinking. "No. If it turns out to be local, we should try to explore more of the station. Sofie meets with Llewelyn, and we go as far as needed to find the scope of the interference. Then we all go back to the case room."

It was a solid plan, but Sofie couldn't lose most of her team to exploring. "Nhu, is there any way identify the loops?"

"Not alone," they said.

Sofie bit her lips on the curses that rumbled up from the dark parts of her mind. "Okay. Amanda, your suggestion is good, but I want you back at the case room helping Nhu. Rick can make his way to the front Temporaries and then back. I'll go talk to Llewelyn. He needs to hear about this."

If Amanda and Nhu could analyze the feeds for repetition, they would know the exact extent of the interference.

"You have your stunner?" Rick asked.

"Always, now go." Sofie kept the call to Nhu open as she walked toward the bullpen. "Nhu, let me know as soon as you find out anything." She held her breath waiting for Nhu to react like an Executive, not a team member.

"Of course. Be careful."

Sofie heard a muffled roar of voices as soon as she stepped into the last intersection before the bullpen, then a wave of pressure rolled over her body as she crossed a security barrier. When she was through, the roar hit full volume.

She pressed her body against a unit door to avoid notice, but no one was looking her way. The street was filled with people, all facing the square in front of the bullpen. Now that she was inside the containment, Sofie could hear more than voices. The smack of flesh against flesh, the high whine of an overloaded stunner, and a scream told her everything she needed to know.

She didn't need to go closer. The authorities were handling it and she would only cause more chaos by coming in from the rear.

Sofie lifted her pad and said, "Nhu?"

No answer. The security screen was blocking the network. Sofie turned and passed back through the barrier.

"Nhu?"

"I'm here. You went dark. What happened?"

"Riot. If you can't see it, then the bullpen feeds are on a loop. I'm coming back."

"Support feeds seem to be live," Nhu said. "Amanda has not appeared on my screens yet. I looked outside our door, and the screens show normal activity, but I saw empty streets."

"I'll try to get Llewelyn on the pad. Call them back to base. I'll be there in ten."

"I will keep watch for any changes." Nhu ended the call.

All of this had happened in the few hours they'd been figuring out how to solve the case. Sofie held up her pad to call Llewelyn. *Fuck, this is not at all discreet. We need wrist comms.* A problem for when they got back.

Llewelyn answered before the first tone ended. "This better be urgent."

"I saw. Two things. Are we truly on our own? You'll have

this under control soon and I don't want to find our authority taken away because you have time to pay attention."

"Resolving this won't free up time, Sofie," he said. "This is the first riot; I don't think it's even close to the last. I won't take away your authority until we have peace."

He must know I'm recording. Sofie chose not to remind him in case he told her to erase the file. She gave him the information they had on the newsfeeds.

"Fuck me. Okay, I can get someone to look into it here. Let me know if you find out who, or why, or how, or any fucking thing." He ended the call.

16

B ack in the case room, Sofie glanced at the screens. Whoever was manipulating them would stop soon if they wanted to keep their actions secret. The longer the images looped, the more likely someone would notice. "Any change?"

"I have not been able to trace the source of the hack," Nhu said. "That is less important now. We must move somewhere safe."

Amanda and Rick found some urgent tasks tidying up the already neat piles of belongings on the shelf.

"We can't move," Sofie said, reminding herself to keep the argument to facts. Nhu, even if they agreed on dropping castes, was afraid, and might try to pull rank if they saw an opening. The case room also had the benefit of being no one's home territory. It would be worse if they moved into some part of the police headquarters. "We need to be where the action is to have any hope of understanding what's really going on."

"We may end up locked inside," Nhu said. They looked to the others for support.

"I don't think there's a good answer here, Nhu," Rick said. "Here or in a less disrupted section, we still have a case to solve."

His answer didn't convince Nhu. Rick didn't seem to care; he went back to his pad and started typing. Sofie wasn't sure if he was pretending or actually finding the team some way to move forward on the case.

"Amanda," Nhu said, "you must agree we will have a better chance to maintain our communications in a safer location."

Sofie hoped Amanda wouldn't say yes.

"Sorry, Nhu," Amanda said, taking her eyes off her pad. "We need to be here. If we're careful, no one will find us. But we don't have the time to move, even if it gets more dangerous. Everything we do must be to solve the case." She returned to whatever she'd been doing before.

"Nhu, we are more likely to be shut out of the action in Executive. That will happen no matter where we move the case room," Sofie said. "Even if we agreed with you, right now no one is here to transport the equipment."

Nhu's face tightened. They were trying to take control of their reaction. Sofie sympathized. Fear was likely a foreign emotion to them. Or physical fear, at least. Working with the Elite families must cause some anxiety, even for Nhu.

They looked at the screens and then their body hardened. "I see. If I told you we could take one of the Elite residences, and I could transfer the data without the equipment, I suppose it would not change your mind?"

"We would still be too far from the section," Sofie said. "We're safe in here, Nhu. You don't have to leave the units."

Nhu pursed their lips and relaxed a fraction. "Very well. I think it is important to call the people you list as contacts.

If reality is so vital, we must gather as much of it as possible."

As if reality is a commodity. It probably is to an Executive.

17

———

"We need to know who's around to help us," Sofie said as Amanda and Rick, apparently finished with their nonexistent chores, rejoined them at the table.

Amanda tossed wrist comms to everyone. "We can't keep pulling out our pads when we're on the streets. These are fully charged."

"Is there anyone else to add to the list?" Sofie said, snapping her comm to her sleeve.

She nodded up to the list of contacts. No one said anything. Maybe this time nothing would come along to drag them away from this task.

"Let's limit our time to fifteen minutes," Rick suggested. "We can't waste time tracking down everyone who doesn't answer."

Sofie had three people to contact, Bindes, Petra, and Torque. If she couldn't talk to them within fifteen minutes, then they were gone like the Elite, or they were dead, or too busy to talk. She nodded and then moved to the second unit for some privacy.

She leaned against the wall and called Bindes. He might not be the contact with the most information, but he knew her medical history.

"Busy, Detective."

"I know. Are you safe?"

"The Open Pit is no longer a bar," he said. "Fully equipped medical center and fortress."

If the same people were with him as last week, Sofie agreed. Large, powerful men and women who were also fully trained medics meant he was protected against anyone trying to take medical supplies — or him.

"If I need you?"

"Only in an emergency," he said. "You remember the back way in?"

The last time she'd left the Open Pit was with an escort through a completely illegal rear door. "Yes."

"I'll leave your name with the guard. How are you?"

Not an easy question to answer. "I'm tired and sometimes think I've missed an important clue. But I have no idea if it's because of the situation or the procedure."

"You should be completely healed physically," he said. "Any headaches?"

"No."

"Dizzy?"

"Not since early yesterday."

"Then you should be well. If any of those symptoms happen, come to me."

"If you have any information for me, will you call?"

"Sofie, I'm cut off here. I know there was a riot because one of my medics came in and told me. I couldn't find any reference on the feeds."

She passed on the information about the tampering.

"Just assume everything is going to shit unless someone you trust tells you otherwise. Or you see it for yourself."

"Will do. It means I won't be much help to you because I should focus on any potential patients."

"Be safe." She ended the call and reached out to Torque.

"Sofie. Can't talk. I'm arranging for the product to be cleared. And then all personnel under my watch. The other managers are doing the same."

"You're leaving?" Of course his employers would want him off a station about to explode.

"Not permanently, according to the corporation. But no idea when they'll let us back."

If he was about to abandon the Mallet, he'd be no use and her information would be of no value to him. "Hope it's soon," she said. "Be safe."

"You too." He ended the call.

Sofie checked with Rick and Amanda. No one had information they could use. Everyone was hunkering down for the duration.

"I have one more call," she said.

"I've got two," Amanda said. "I'm not hopeful."

"I'm done," Rick said.

"Did anyone know about the newsfeed looping?"

"No, and no weird reactions like I'd caught someone up to no good," Amanda said. "This isn't being done by the usual assholes."

"Amanda, help Nhu when you're done," Sofie said. "Rick, check our supplies and weapons. I have a feeling we're stuck with what we have, but we need to know exactly what that is."

Sofie hit the contact for Petra Starlight. She'd been the one to find a vital clue in the last investigation. Maybe she'd do the same now.

"Petra?" Sofie asked when the call was answered but no one spoke.

"One moment, Sofie." Petra sounded harried.

A legitimate clinic might actually be a few steps behind the illegal ones in preparing, Sofie thought.

"Okay. What do you want from me? Or have for me, I guess," Petra asked.

Sofie updated her on the problem with the information streaming to the public. "It means you need to have a way to verify everything," she said.

"And here I thought you were calling to give me good news," Petra said. "It's good to know. I'll send a message to all clinics to make sure they're safe. Anything else?"

A million things. "Are you safe?"

"We were operating as usual until your call. I'll make sure we've pulled down the security doors. I'll call in all the doctors. How bad is it?"

"The riot outside the police station was bad. My captain will bring it under control, but you might want to work on the assumption that official help is tied up."

"The police station is too close to Support," Petra said. "Should I ask for the private security people to help out?"

"The Elites are gone, Petra. I don't know if the private security is still around." *I should have told Bindes that little fact.*

"They can't do that," Petra said. "The Elites, I mean."

"They have. If you think you need muscle, I can ask someone to send a few people." Maybe the boss of the dark streets would help.

"Unless you can send people to every clinic, don't bother. How widely known is it that the Elite have left?"

"We're keeping it close," Sofie said. "No need for the rioters to find out there's no oversight."

"You need to stop this, Sofie," Petra said.

"I will." Sofie ended the call and sent the update to Bindes about the Elites.

18

None of their contacts had any information to share. It seemed like the residents of the Mallet were either gathering to tear down the hierarchy or hunkering down to outlast the upheaval. If no one took control soon, they would die in their units — which might be for the best. Whoever told Torque he was leaving temporarily could have lied. Sofie couldn't think why; surely anyone would be willing to leave the Mallet if given the opportunity.

"Did you find the tampering with the newsfeeds?" Sofie asked.

She wanted to be outside the room tracking down the person who was driving people to destroy the station. All her years of experience didn't stop that feeling. What kept her inside was the lack of a lead. They had nothing but problems. No way to see what was really happening, no support from the police, no idea why anyone would want to cause the chaos.

Nhu didn't look up from the information on their pad.

"Not completely," Amanda said. "It's happening at the broadcast point. So, the drones are sending their images to whoever owns them, and those people are still sending updates as usual. Some program is shunting the live images to storage and sending out loops."

"Try to turn the redirect program off," Sofie said. "It might only benefit us to see the action on the streets, but we need it."

"Yeah. Surprising no one noticed," Rick said.

"Not if you think about it," Amanda said, still typing. "People locked inside have no way of knowing the images are recorded. I guess unless they see themselves on the screen. But unlikely. The people going to work or coming back — there must be at least a few people on all the production lines so they don't shut down completely — are on the streets and not worried about what's supposed to be happening wherever they are."

"They will if a riot heads their way," Sofie said. "But yeah. If the riots are contained to sites with little traffic, no one will notice them. And if the people who are supposed to inform us of the news don't check their output, they won't notice."

"And they are too busy to go look at screens?" Rick asked.

"The screens in the media units show what the drones send in, not what the street screens display," Amanda said. "I need to concentrate; this program is tied into most of the Mallet's communications."

Sofie sat at the table looking at her blank screen. Rick joined her, facing the projections on the wall.

"We're going to get pulled away from our purpose," Rick said. "We should put it up there, our orders."

"To stop whoever is provoking the disruption?" Sofie woke her pad and sent the words to a blank space on the wall. "Or have I already lost sight of it?"

"No, that's what Llewelyn told us to do," Rick said. "But we haven't found a single lead with that, and now we're trying to solve a problem with communications that we could hand over to anyone in the media."

Sofie stared at the wall, trying to find anything that proved Rick was wrong. He wasn't. "Yeah. We keep trying to get a name or a lead. One of the leaders who organized the riot. The way someone gets instructions, anything. But we keep jumping on the crisis in front of us."

"You want Amanda to stop?" Rick asked.

If she had any other tasks for Amanda, Sofie would tell her to send the information to every media group. To call and alert them so no one could divert her message, and then stop working on the problem. "Maybe we should look at why someone is doing this," she said to avoid making a decision. "The *why* might lead to the *how*. I know we might end up off course, but we have nothing else."

"And Amanda?" Rick asked. "She'd be good at figuring out motives."

Sofie typed *Why, How, Who*, under the goal and then closed her pad. "Amanda, if you can't shut it down in the next fifteen minutes, pass it on."

"Okay," Amanda said.

"Power up your pads," Sofie said. "If we get a lead, I want our equipment ready to go."

She handed Rick her pad and stunner. He gathered the other devices and placed them on the chargers.

Nhu looked up from their pad, pulling it away as Rick reached for it. "I'm plugged in. And I'm not going on the streets."

Sofie shook her head at Rick when he looked at her for direction. "Nhu's right. So, why would someone take the Mallet to the brink? Or destroy it like this, rather than blow it up?"

"I think I know," Nhu said.

19

"What?" Rick asked as Nhu drew out the pause. How could he be so blunt and impatient when talking to an Executive? Sofie tried to treat Nhu as an equal, but too many years of being afraid of accidentally offending a member of a higher caste made it hard to change in a moment. Although perhaps it wasn't her fear of a reprimand that held her back. Her fear of anyone finding out she suffered from the Fades was stronger, and she'd carried it since she was a child.

Something to dig into if we survive the current crisis.

"It's in the contract," Nhu said. They looked up from the pad in their hands. "Why do you stay on the Mallet?"

"I owe on my contract," Rick said. "If I could pay it out, I'd be gone."

"Same," Amanda said. "Is there any other reason?"

"Isn't that why everyone stays?" Sofie asked. In the past, she couldn't leave because of her condition. Meds to control the Fades were expensive, if available at all, off the station. "I mean, anyone who can't survive off the Mallet would have to stay, but other than that, anyone would go, right? Why do you stay?"

Nhu smiled at the question. "You assume we in the Executive carry no debts. My family was not always Executive. In the past, you could buy your way into a higher caste. With debt or favors, of course, because the cost to buy in free and clear was out of reach for any resident."

"How long ago?" Amanda asked, finally looking up from her pad. "I don't remember hearing about this."

"The Elites control what is taught in school. I am the seventh generation of Eckerman Executives. I still owe a debt of far more than I or four generations of my descendants could hope to clear. I will be required to produce three offspring to ensure the debt is not lost."

"They don't do that to us," Rick said. "If we don't have kids, our debt dies with us."

Nhu laughed. "You think they didn't store your reproductive matter? If you do not produce heirs, they will be produced for you."

Just when I think life on the Mallet can't get more fucked up. Any kid of mine would inherit my condition. Another problem to fix when this is over.

"And the Elites? Do they owe someone?" Sofie asked.

"When the Mallet last changed leadership, the Elites were savvy in negotiating the contract," Nhu said. "They ensured that they were free of debt. They hoped it would allow them freedom to come and go."

"And did it?" Amanda asked. "Or I guess the question is, why do the Elites stay on the station?"

"Exactly," Nhu said. "I have always accepted that they do it out of a need to control. However, the Elites were not the only clever people when it came to creating the contract.

There is a clause that requires them to reside on the station to maintain their ownership."

"And they are gone," Sofie said. "Who runs the Mallet now?"

"Surprising, but it is still the Elite families," Nhu said. "There is a ten standard-day grace period. Perhaps someone anticipated our current position. A short time when the Elites could withdraw for safety reasons."

"How long have they been gone?" Amanda asked. She held up her hand to stop the reply and typed on her pad. "Sorry about that. I just handed the comms problem over to the media people. This is far more important."

Nhu nodded like an indulgent parent. "Yes, we will need all our attention on this clause in the contract. I believe it is critical to resolving this situation. The Elite families have been off the Mallet four days."

"Okay, let me think this through," Sofie said. "The Elites have abandoned their position. That means their income is cut off. No one is in charge, so if we can get the residents to talk to each other instead of fighting, we can set up a new hierarchy."

"Perhaps," Nhu said. "I find it difficult to believe we have been abandoned. This station is too lucrative for anyone to simply walk away."

"I've never thought about it before, but how can the Elites own the station?" Sofie asked. "They didn't build it. They didn't buy it from anyone."

Nhu pressed their lips together before answering. Something they didn't know?

"I cannot find a definitive answer," Nhu said. "It may be simply they assumed the role after so much time in charge. But it doesn't matter. As long as someone else thinks they own it, they can sell. No one has corrected them on this point in the past."

"But it could be a takeover," Amanda said. "Get rid of the Elites, and then take the station."

"Yes." Nhu typed something into their pad.

The repercussions overwhelmed Sofie. She tried to order her thoughts and form some useful questions. "Who would take over? The corporations who use the Mallet?"

"The Elites?" Rick said. "If they want to keep control and want off — who doesn't? — then this chaos could be the opening move to renegotiate."

"If they're not forced to live here, the living conditions will not improve," Nhu said. "We need to circumvent whatever plans exist regardless of who intends to take over."

New information, no matter how much it turns our understanding of the universe on its head, doesn't change the fact that we don't know what to do next.

20

"Until the new owners identify themselves," Sofie said, "we have time to change things."

Nhu's pad chimed. They looked down, smiled, and tapped the screen.

"What would happen if we leaked the news about the Elites leaving?" Amanda asked. "I mean yes, chaos, but we have that now."

"Perhaps we can discuss this when Haadiya arrives," Nhu said.

Sofie turned her attention from trying to think of an answer to Amanda's question that didn't involve some version of catastrophe, and stared at Nhu. "How does he know where we are?"

"I invited him," Nhu said. "I can't leave him out there to be killed."

"How many others did you inform of our highly secret location?" Amanda asked. "And why did you do anything without talking to us first?"

The shock on Nhu's face at Amanda's tone told Sofie how delicate the agreement to drop the castes was in reality. Nhu still acted like they were an Executive. Making decisions and keeping secrets. Sofie waited for them to answer.

Nhu's expression hardened. "I will not abandon my caste. Haadiya is a friend. Or as much of one as is possible at our level."

"How many more?" Sofie asked. "You think the space is too small already, now you've added Haadiya."

"No others," Nhu said. "I thought he hid with the others, but he answered my call when I reached out for help."

So, they are willing to let the rest of their caste fend for themselves just to take a sip more power when we win?

Having another Executive on the team might be an advantage. Rick could deal with keeping Haadiya in line, but Nhu was Sofie's problem. "You can't make decisions like this without telling us," she said. "You agreed that we would drop the castes until this was over. Did you change your mind?"

Completely abandoning her fear of offending people in power would take time, but this was a great first step. Respectful and calm words should work better than what she wanted to do — scream at Nhu to stop getting in the way and do as they were told.

"Dropping castes is more complicated than simply pretending we are all equal," Nhu said after a moment. "I am unused to working on a team. I will not apologize for doing what I thought was right, but perhaps I understand more now that surprises are not welcome."

"When can we expect Haadiya to arrive?" Sofie asked, deciding to accept the weak explanation because she couldn't see any benefit in continuing. The damage was already done. "Someone will bring him up-to-date."

"Within five minutes," Nhu said.

Sofie looked over at Rick. "Go wait for him and make sure he's alone before you let him in."

Sofie turned back to Nhu and Amanda. "We need a lead. Until this is all settled, we are all one team," Sofie said. "Our focus now is to find out who is instigating the riots. We have a motive. Now we follow whatever trail we can find back to the person or corporation leading this asinine plan. A takeover is one thing, but risking the lives of people forced to stay on the Mallet is another."

"The screens are live again," Amanda said. "Now that the media groups are aware of the problem, they'll monitor it. At least we can see what's really happening out there."

Sofie's pad pinged. A message from Llewelyn. "The riots are shut down for now, but no leader identified yet."

"This is a good time for you to leave and find clues," Nhu said. "Before it all starts again, and you're trapped."

Why are they trying to get rid of us? To give them time to persuade Haadiya to their side of the caste argument? Does it matter?

"We wait for Haadiya," Sofie said. "Let me check with the boss of the dark streets. He might have some names."

No one answered her call.

"Maybe the dark streets are overrun?" Amanda said. "No cameras in there, no drones."

Whatever their agenda, Nhu was right about the team needing to get out of the room and find a lead. It was dangerous, but being a cop on the Mallet meant she faced danger every day. She wasn't happy leaving Nhu alone, but she didn't have the resources to assign a sitter.

"That's the boss's problem to solve for now," Sofie said. "We go out when Haadiya is settled. Any chance we have enough here for disguises? We need to get close to people before they realize we're cops."

"I don't see anything that would work," Amanda said. "We need coveralls, some grease to make us dirty, and few lessons on how to stop walking and breathing like a cop."

"Rick did undercover; he can give us some tips," Sofie said. "You and I can borrow some coveralls from a vacant unit. Rick is going to be hard to fit out from random clothes. There aren't many people in Maintenance his size."

Nhu looked up from their pad. "Your captain can obtain them from the police supplies."

"What supplies?" Sofie asked.

"For undercover operations. I thought you knew. They keep a full wardrobe." Nhu smiled as though to say, *see? I am valuable.* "I can requisition a full set with accessories if you wish."

Okay, so maybe they could be useful as well as trouble. "Accessories?"

"Tools, grease, a spray to simulate the odors created by working hours at a hot machine." Nhu raised an eyebrow. "Would you like me to do it?"

"Yes. And have it left in the bullpen. We can't have deliveries sent here."

———————

21

"He's here," Rick announced as he opened the unit door. "It looks clear outside. Three people watching from the corner."

"My people," Haadiya said. "They will leave now."

Why is it so hard for Executives to understand what the word secret *means? They have enough of them.*

Haadiya dropped a pair of packs into the corner and joined them at the table.

"How long before someone else comes knocking?" Sofie asked.

"They won't talk," Haadiya said. "And if someone comes looking for us, they will be stopped."

The way he said the words didn't leave space for argument.

"Why do you believe that?" Sofie asked.

"Oh, you have changed, Sofie. I do approve of your new forthrightness. All will be clear in a moment. What progress have you made?" He looked at the wall of screens. "Oh, very little."

"If we don't keep getting interrupted, we might solve the

case," she said. "What do you know?"

"Sofie believes we are all equal until this mess blows over," Nhu said.

"Oh, I disagree," Haadiya said. "We are all special in our own way. I, for instance, would have no idea how to start an investigation."

A brief scowl marred Nhu's face. "You might find that attitude difficult to maintain."

"We don't have time for this," Amanda said. "We drop the caste expectations. We don't carry grudges, and we don't invite anyone here. We're sure that this is all about a takeover of the Mallet. Did I miss anything, Sofie?"

"No, I think you covered the important points. Settle in here, Haadiya. We're going to pick up a few things."

"What about secrets?" Haadiya said. "Not mundane things, but big, important things. Truths that may assist in resolving our current troubles."

"Spit it out," Sofie said.

He smiled like they were at a social event, and he didn't want to offend anyone with an opinion. "I am the boss of the dark streets." Haadiya nodded his head and Sofie thought he was giving them permission to accept him as someone vital to their mission.

"Yeah," Rick said. "You control the worst section of the Mallet."

"No need for sarcasm, Rick." Haadiya pulled out his pad. "Sofie, please try the contact you were given for the boss."

Sofie weighed her feelings. He always gave her an asshole vibe, but the boss had helped her in the past. And now, as she thought back, there really was no reason the boss would know anything about her. She took her pad off the charger and stared at him as she hit the contact number.

Haadiya's pad chimed. "Oh, Sofie dear. How may I help you save the Mallet?"

She stared at him, unable to accept what he'd announced, even with the proof.

"What the fuck," Rick said. "How long?"

"All my life," Haadiya said. "Although I suppose I've only held the title of boss for just over twenty years."

Amanda's pad pinged. "The disguises are waiting in the bullpen. I should go get them. Maybe I can hack us some more access levels while I'm on a dedicated pad."

"Good idea," Sofie said. "Just wait until we learn how an Executive liaison became the boss of the dark streets." Some instinct told her to believe Haadiya, but it didn't make him a good guy.

"I will give you the short version," Haadiya said. "My family created the dark streets. Before we took control, the crimes were spread over the Mallet. No street was safe from thugs, drug dealers or prostitutes. Desperate people were left to die, and some even made their way to end their misery in front of Elite homes. I suppose they were making a statement."

So, instead of making life a little easier, the Elites just crammed the problem into a corner and ignored it. Sofie didn't remember the Mallet the way Haadiya described it. So this must have started hundreds of years ago. Even if the Elites scrubbed it from history, people would have talked for a generation or two about the bad old days, keeping the story alive. Or, maybe the memories only stuck until the next horror took their attention from the past.

"Anyway. My great-great-grandfather was the first boss. He wanted to buy his way into their caste. They offered him this instead. Rather than being the head of the tenth Elite family, he could be the king of his own domain. He agreed. I mean, what could he have done? The Elites would never have allowed him to join them."

"So, your great-great-grandfather developed a benevolent environment for the worst of the Mallet residents?" Nhu asked.

"No. Until my father took over, it was simply contained mayhem. But he was more enlightened. Living and working in the dark streets became an identity with value. You might still have performed degrading acts, but you were protected. You no longer needed to fight for every morsel of food. You were given a place to report abuse. Order of a kind was restored."

"And now you think you have a shot at becoming an Elite?" Rick asked. "Enough time has passed and maybe they'll let you buy in?"

Sofie was surprised at the level of bitterness in Rick's words. Did he see Haadiya's secret as a personal betrayal?

"So what does all that mean for saving the Mallet?" Sofie asked. "The Elites abandoned us, so I guess your dream of becoming one of them is gone. How can you help?"

"I have never wanted to join them," Haadiya said. "In truth, I think they are feeding on the misery of the residents. I offer far more to my people than the Elites offer even to the Executive. However, I have been happy to give them the impression I was ambitious. The current generation have no idea of my real identity."

"And how can you help?" Sofie asked again. She couldn't afford to be sidetracked by an interesting story. The Mallet was being attacked. "I mean, more than offering information from your people on the street. People who had no idea someone had tampered with the newsfeeds. People who have not provided one single piece of information."

"Perhaps I will reconsider my approval of the new attitude," he said. "I have safe passage markers for you. They will get you through the dark streets. I have directed all my people to focus only on finding intelligence and reporting it in. We have to save the Mallet, Sofie, but we must also think of the future. Who will control us when this nightmare ends?"

22

The revelation from Haadiya didn't change the fact that they needed to get the case solved. Sofie took the black token from him and tucked it into a pocket. "Let's hope your people get some names for us," she said.

"We can't worry about the future of the Mallet," Nhu said. "First we save it, then we deal with keeping it profitable."

There was some reason Nhu hadn't found a way to leave with the Elites. They had no ties here, and there must be a shuttle somewhere taking passengers that they could bribe their way onto. Maybe not a comfortable trip, but away from possible death. Being on the station when the violence was over put them in a good position to become a leader, but there was no guarantee.

"We still need to go undercover," Amanda said. "It's great we have spies, but we can't be stuck here waiting."

Sofie glanced at the screens. "Can you contact your spies, Haadiya?"

He shook his head. "It would put them in too much danger."

"It's quiet out there right now," Sofie said. "Anything happening around the bullpen?"

Amanda switched the newsfeed view to the drones. "Crowded, but in control."

"I will need some supplies from my home," Nhu said. "I did not expect to be in such tight quarters for so long."

It has only been about six hours. How quickly were they anticipating a solution?

"Rick, Nhu should have an escort," Sofie said. "Don't take too long."

"I'll go get the disguises," Amanda said. "I can do a few things on the official databases from the office. Things that could be traced, so I can't do them here and expect to explain it away."

So that leaves me with Haadiya. The thought didn't bother her as much as it would have a day ago. He had a reason to be on the Mallet. If he was to be believed, he wanted to keep his people safe, no matter how grim their lives were.

"Does someone need to stay inside this room?" Haadiya asked. "Now that I see it, like Nhu I regret not bringing certain items."

"We need someone in here at all times," Sofie said. "I can't have us coming back to find the place ransacked."

"Then I guess it's you right now," Rick said. "While we're out, I'll take a look at the extra units. Make sure they're secure enough to hold a prisoner."

Sofie couldn't think of a reason to force anyone to stay instead of her. Alone, she could assess her health. Maybe take a nap without anyone knowing. Think through the possible avenues to investigate. "No more than an hour. If you get in trouble, I want to know."

"Follow us on the screens," Amanda said. "I can key our trackers to automatically send the closest drone feed to a screen."

If they could trust the feeds, it was a perfect way to keep the investigation going without having to check in all the time. "Do it," Sofie said. "I can give you a heads up if problems come close."

In a moment she was alone.

She scanned the screens. Busy but calm. It wouldn't take much to turn a crowd into a riot, but right now everyone should be safe.

She opened her pad to the medical scanner. She felt healthy, but feeling it wasn't enough. Time to get some real information about her recovery. She placed her palm on the screen and initiated the tests.

Heart rate, normal. Temperature, within normal range. Blood oxygen, normal. Proceed to step two.

Sofie looked at the light in the center of the pad and blinked when it flickered.

Reaction time, normal. Proceed to step three.

The last step of the scan was a series of four puzzles designed to check her cognitive power.

Thought processes normal.

Normal for her. In the past, Sofie had made sure that she was medicated immediately before taking a scan to keep the results consistent. So these results meant her healing phase was over. Now all she had left to do was convince herself not to worry that she'd collapse in an emergency. Not easy after more than forty years of anxiety.

She cleared her pad. Time to figure out how to stay functional without sleep. Now that she was healthy, it was the same way everyone else did it — stims and determination.

The screens showed three paths. Nhu and Rick were

almost at the Executive section. With luck, Nhu's extra supplies would be small. Amanda was already at the bullpen. Haadiya was somewhere near the Temporaries. Importantly, there was no violence on the station.

Watching other people working didn't take much attention. Sofie wondered about Haadiya's comment about the future of the Mallet. It didn't make sense that the contract would be broken immediately if the Elites left the Mallet, and ten days seemed sufficient to resolve any problem. But there were only a little over five days left, and the situation was getting worse. How were they planning to retain control? Was there a secure location holding one representative of each family so they could prove the Mallet wasn't abandoned?

The residency clause did make sense. When the residents of the Mallet agreed on the caste system, they wanted to motivate the leaders to maintain living conditions to a minimum standard. If she was wrong and they'd abandoned their positions, why?

She started making notes to answer the question. They knew something that would hamper profitability of the Mallet. They were being pressured by a client to hand over the reins. They had a plan she couldn't figure out because she thought like a cop, not an Elite.

She projected the notes onto a screen and moved her attention back to the situation outside.

Rick and Nhu were already back from Executive and checking out the units they'd use as cells. All clear for them.

Haadiya was in Maintenance, and it was quiet. His lieutenants likely cleared the way for him.

Amanda. Fuck! The drone feed showed a riot in her location. How had that gone out of control in the minute she'd taken her eyes off the screen?

She tapped her comm. "Amanda?"

"I'm almost there."

23

S ofie messaged Rick to stay in place. If the riot behind Amanda grew, it would be on top of the case room fast. Haadiya acknowledged her warning but said he would be fine no matter what.

The unit door opened, and Amanda fell through, landing on her knees. Blood seeped through her pant leg, and she held her chest tight.

Sofie slammed the door and helped Amanda lower herself to the floor with her back against a wall.

"How bad?" Sofie asked as she checked the obvious slash on Amanda's leg.

"Broken rib. Another cut to my side."

The medi kit wouldn't be enough to heal any of her wounds. Sofie opened it anyway, pulled out a pain suppressant, and spilled the bandages onto the floor for easy reach.

"I lost the disguises," Amanda said. "We need to try again."

"Fuck disguises," Sofie muttered. "Let me get at the wounds."

Amanda released her arms and blood seeped down her

side. Sofie passed Amanda the pain meds and then apologized. "This is going to hurt anyway."

"I know," Amanda said. She bit down on the capsule and closed her eyes. "Just do it, okay?"

The wound on Amanda's leg had stopped bleeding. It needed attention, but not as much as the one under her arm. "I need to take off your jacket."

She slid the point of a pair of scissors under the hem of the jacket and started cutting. Amanda's body tightened, but she didn't scream. The wound was an inch below Amanda's armpit. Sofie grabbed a pack of wadding and pressed the material into the cut. "Hold it there until I get the coagulant open."

Tears squeezed out of Amanda's closed eyes, but she lowered her arm to hold the wad in place. The container for the coagulant was airtight. Sofie pressed the seal and waited for the lid to pop. It seemed like forever, but Sofie knew it was only a few seconds. Keeping the contents dry was far more important than speed. Damp powder wouldn't do its job.

"Can you lie on your side?" Sofie asked. If Amanda's ribs were broken, movement could puncture her lung, but the location of the wound was awkward.

The wadding fell out as Amanda slid to the side and raised her arm, breathing hard.

Now that the wound was exposed, Sofie could see it wasn't as life threatening as she feared — but bad enough that it needed stitches. A doctor might disagree with her, though. She shook the coagulant onto the surface of the hole and watched as it formed a bloody crust. The temporary scab would have to hold long enough for her to get Amanda more help.

"I'll go find a medic," she said. "Let me tape up your leg."

Amanda opened her eyes and took a shallow breath. "It's dangerous out there."

"I'll be careful. Where do your ribs hurt the most?"

Amanda pointed to where a bruise was forming below the laceration.

"Is the suppressant working?" Sofie asked as she finished applying the tape to Amanda's leg.

"It's taking the edge off," Amanda muttered. "Just do what you need to do."

Sofie kept her eyes locked on Amanda's as she gently probed at the center of bruise. Amanda didn't flinch.

"Nothing's moving," Sofie said. "Probably bruised or cracked, not broken."

"That's fine, then." Amanda tried to smile but it turned into a grimace. "I'll be okay. No need to go looking for a doctor."

"Nope. Where's your pad?"

Amanda nodded toward a pocket in her jacket on the side closest to the floor. "Help me upright."

Sofie moved to Amanda's less damaged side and pushed her up to sitting. She took Amanda's pad and told her to open it.

"When was the last time you did a health check?" Probably longer ago than Sofie, but maybe healthy people checked regularly, too.

"Month ago."

Sofie opened the medical scanner and helped Amanda place her hand on the screen.

The readouts started to pop up fast, and none of them were green.

Dangerous level of blood loss. Pressure low. Temperature low. Heartbeat low. Transport to clinic immediately.

Sofie showed Amanda the screen. "I'm going for help."

"Where?" Amanda asked.

At least she wasn't arguing with the scanner. "I have a few places. I'll be careful. First, let's get you comfortable."

"I need to know where," Amanda said. "Get me on a chair so I can watch the screens and make sure you don't run into trouble."

"How did you get hurt?" Sofie asked, hoping to distract Amanda.

"I was on my way back. It came out of nowhere. I got pushed and fell, then someone kicked me. Boots had spikes. I rolled away before it got worse."

"I'm sorry I didn't see it coming," Sofie said. "I should have been able to divert you."

Amanda grabbed Sofie's hand. "It all happened too fast. Get me on the chair. Tell me where you plan to go."

Sofie couldn't see any way of convincing Amanda to stay where she was, safe on the floor with no possibility of falling. "Okay. Tell me how to help you up."

In the end Amanda used Sofie as a post, doing most of the work to get herself to her feet. They stumbled together to the closest chair. Sofie was covered in blood by the time Amanda was firmly seated at the table.

"Can't go out like this," she said. She washed the blood from her hands and then grabbed a spare outfit from her pack.

"Where are you going?" Amanda asked again. Her voice was steadier now.

"I have a couple of options," Sofie said. "I'll try Petra in Support."

"You can't bring a Support doctor through this," Amanda said.

"We'll see," Sofie said. "I have another contact in Maintenance if I need it. Just try to stay alive long enough for me to get back."

24

Despite what she told Amanda, Sofie wasn't sure she'd be safe. Knowing a riot could take her by surprise meant she'd be more vigilant, but if Amanda was taken down so easily, nothing could keep her safe.

The closest spare unit to the case room was one street over and half a street down. There was no action on the screen, so she should be safe getting that far. A few minutes checking with the rest of the team and talking to Petra Starlight wouldn't put Amanda's life at any more risk than it was already. Running around the Mallet looking for help could take longer than Amanda had.

She checked her stunner was fully charged, and slapped on a wrist com. "Don't make anything worse," she said to Amanda before checking the screens to make sure the street was clear.

It took her three minutes to get to the spare unit. No one accosted her on the way, but the streets were no longer empty.

She closed the door behind her and turned on the lights.

The unit was bare. The bathroom closet was still in place, but the kitchen was ripped out and not in a way any self-respecting builder would do it. Someone had vandalized the unit. Not recently, though, and right now that was all that mattered. The unit was secure. She had connection to the network, and privacy.

First, she reached out to Rick and brought him up to date. "Amanda will be okay for now," she said. "Get back when you can do it safely. I don't need more patients."

"We don't have screens, so I'm going to do a little recon before we move," Rick said. "This unit is bare, what's yours like?"

"Same. Not sure how we're supposed to interrogate anyone if we ever get a lead. But it will work for a holding cell." She checked her pad for news. "Any idea if Support is safe?"

"It was when we came through. It's like a different world up front," Rick said.

"Like when it was just protests?" Sofie asked. A few days ago, when Maintenance was riddled with protests, the Support section didn't even have news about it on their screens. "If they don't have a clue about the riots, they won't be preparing."

"I have made sure they are informed," Nhu's voice came through the comm.

"Thank you," Sofie said. "Have you heard from Haadiya?"

"Yeah, he's making his way back with his lieutenants providing security," Rick said. "I can ask him to lend you a few people."

Did she want an escort? If Petra said she would come, or send one of her doctors, yes. "I'll ask him myself if I need it. When you get back let me know how Amanda is doing."

When Rick signed off, Sofie placed her call to Petra Starlight.

"Yes, Detective?" Petra said.

"I need someone to give medical aid to a colleague." Sofie described the injuries and what actions she'd taken.

"Bring her in," Petra said. "You should be able to get an ambulance to come with a float gurney."

"I can't take that chance," Sofie said. "The streets aren't safe for anyone who can't run."

"I can't spare a doctor and equipment if that's the case," Petra said. "I'm sorry, Sofie. I have to think of the people who need my help here."

"How are you coping?" Sofie needed to know that someone was making plans for an outbreak of violence.

"We got the message," Petra said. "I'm coordinating the Support clinics. I think someone is working in Executive. They aren't as isolated from this as they hoped. Your Maintenance clinics should be asking for help if they need it."

The doctors would probably be doing just that unless they decided to abandon their clinics. She wouldn't be surprised if some had already gone into hiding.

"If I can get my hands on some supplies, do you think you could walk me through the treatment?"

"Stitching a wound is simply sewing," Petra said. "From what you tell me, there may be internal bleeding. I can't help you do anything about that. You must get her to a clinic."

"Okay. I have another alternative," Sofie said. "Be safe." *Why did I think someone of a higher caste would put herself in danger for a cop?*

Acknowledging the pettiness of her thoughts didn't reduce her disappointment.

25

W hy did she still want to keep Bindes a secret? It wouldn't be odd that Sofie had contacts in the murky world of off-the-books clinics. But she couldn't get rid of the feeling that her medical history would become public. There was no basis for this fear, but it was real, and now wasn't the time for introspection. Later, when this situation was solved, she'd work it out and find a way to drop her lifelong paranoia.

Just going to the Open Pit was a risk. If Bindes wasn't there, she'd waste time. So, Sofie called him.

"Busy right now," Bindes said. "Is there a problem with your recovery since we last talked?"

"I'm fine," Sofie said, for the first time believing it. "I have a problem. One of my colleagues needs medical attention."

"You have official clinics for that," Bindes said. "I'm the only place where people in this section can be sure of help no matter what side they're on."

She couldn't tell him anything about their task force, but she also couldn't risk taking Amanda to the nearest clinic. If it was possible, she would already be there. "Except if they're cops? She's badly hurt."

Bindes didn't answer immediately. Was that a good sign?

"What's her condition?"

Sofie told him about the readings and her examination. "I don't know what else to do."

"You stopped the bleeding. That's the most important thing. I can't come, Sofie, but I can send someone. Where are you?"

"No, I'll come to you." She'd figure out a way to bring the medic to their case room and swear them to secrecy.

"Can you bring her med scan?" Bindes asked.

"Yes." She could have Amanda send the results along. And since Bindes was treating anyone who needed it, maybe he would know who was leading the riots and she'd get him to spill face-to-face. "I have a few questions, too."

She ended the call before he could say anything else. The trip to the Open Pit would be faster through the dark streets. And she had the token from Haadiya. Perhaps she'd ask for an escort on the way back.

She contacted Amanda. "I need the scan results."

"Okay. I'll do another before I send it. Maybe I'm getting better without help."

She sounded stronger, but that might just be from sitting in a chair and not stressing the wounds. "Rick and Nhu should be there at some point. He knows the situation. Haadiya is on his way too. Just hang on."

"Sure, I was just waiting for you to tell me to do that," Amanda said.

"Good to hear you have some attitude," Sofie said.

"It's hard to be reasonable in this much pain. I wish I'd asked you to leave another dose near me."

Too much painkiller could cause problems. "Ask Rick

when he gets there," Sofie said. "I'm leaving here in a second. I might not be able to respond to messages until I'm back with you."

"So no change from the usual," Amanda said.

Sofie laughed and ended the call. She felt for the token in her pocket. Going to the dark streets under the protection of the boss felt much more secure than just getting safe passage through once she was inside. The thought made her realize how many allies she had in this crisis, both people she expected and some who came as a surprise. The caste system blocked her ability to see people, rather than jobs. Maybe it was that way all over the Mallet.

THE PATH to the dark streets led through part of Maintenance. Sofie fought the urge to race through the streets, knowing it would bring attention. Running also meant she wouldn't be fully alert to the warning signs of trouble.

The sound of voices rolled in from the side streets, but only voices — no breaking fixtures, no screams of pain. Not yet a mob driven by violence. If it did flash into a riot, Sofie had nowhere to go, because the noise came from all sides.

She kept close to the storefronts and unit doors as she slipped through the streets. If the crowd was small, she wouldn't get trapped. If it was big enough to push her against the wall and pin her down, it would be out of control, and nothing her team did would stop the chaos from spreading.

The entrance to the dark streets was a block away when she heard boots rushing toward her. She ran, fumbling the token into her hand and holding it out. Guards blocked her way as usual, but this time, one of the women ran toward Sofie, aiming her stunner.

Sofie held up her hands as she stumbled to a stop.

"Don't be an idiot," the woman rasped. "Get inside before it's too late."

The stunner wasn't aimed at Sofie, but over her shoulder in the direction of the approaching sound. Sofie looked back to see how large the crowd was, but no one was in sight.

The guards parted to let her through. The woman returned to her position at the entrance.

"Put the token away," the woman said. "We know who has them."

Why did Haadiya give them out if no one needed them?

"I'm headed for the Open Pit," Sofie said. "I have to come back this way."

"Three right turns in a row, you'll be a street from the Pit. Can't guarantee you'll be able to leave," the woman said. "Be fast. Our stunners are keeping the assholes away for now. Don't know if that will continue."

Sofie ran. She'd suspected there was an exit close to the bar, because Bindes provided medical attention to the residents of the dark streets.

She came to the end of the street after the third turn and saw why no one outside the dark streets knew about this exit. It looked like a dead end. If she didn't know this was a way out, she'd turn back. But the woman said to go this way.

Sofie used her police override and ducked under the roll-up door before it fully opened. The unit was empty. A second door with a screen showing the street outside faced her.

The street was clear except for one man casually leaning against the wall to the right. His long black coat was doing a poor job of hiding his stunner.

Sofie looked around for a way to let the guard know the door was about to open. But there was nothing. She checked the screen again. The man was staring at her, lips pressed together. The silent message *what are you waiting for?* clear on his face.

Sofie pressed the switch to open the door. It rose a meter and then stopped. She rolled through the space and the door closed again.

"Nothing between here and the Pit," the man said.

Sofie nodded and ran again, trusting his word and questioning why she did. The dark streets seemed more like a community than any other place on the Mallet right now.

26

T he door to the Open Pit was half rolled up. Sofie ducked under and then stood to the side. Someone was saving credits by keeping half the lights off. Coming into the dimness left her blind. A good defense if there were only one or two attackers. A mob would just keep moving forward, damaging whatever they encountered.

"Come on," Bindes said. His voice came from her left.

Sofie blinked and the vague shapes resolved into people. Like the last time she was here, the bar was set up as a medical center. Tables arranged to hold patients rather than drinks. Equipment and supplies arranged close at hand for anyone to reach.

"Before you ask, no casualties yet," Bindes said.

"Let's hope that doesn't change," she said. "What do you have for me? Who am I taking back with me?"

He beckoned her to the office he kept in the back. "Let's do this privately."

Inside the office, he pointed to the narrow examination bed.

"I don't have time," Sofie said. "Amanda needs help now. And I need a name of someone I can talk to. If there's any hope of saving the station, I can't hang around."

"A few minutes. Then you'll know if you need to take precautions."

She gave up arguing when he prodded her and took her temperature.

"You are healthy," he said after checking the results. "I need to talk to your colleague. I'm not prepared to go on secondhand information."

"You have the results of two scans," she said.

"I need to look. Think of it as a way to keep anyone from finding your hideout."

Sofie took his pad and called Amanda. A wrist comm wouldn't give Bindes a big enough area to assess. "I still have to go back through the streets."

"And I want to make sure you take the correct items with you."

"Hey, Sofie," Rick said. "Amanda's a little busy suffering right now."

"The doctor needs to see what the problem is," Sofie said. "I'll let him take over."

Bindes took the pad and started instructing Rick on how to move Amanda without causing more damage.

"Good job on the dressing. Her leg will heal," he said quietly, as if talking to himself. "I need to see the bigger wound."

Sofie glanced at the bare walls as Bindes walked Rick through removing the coagulant scab. She heard Amanda moan. "Can we give her something?" she asked, still not looking at the screen. Acting in an emergency hadn't given her a chance to react to the blood and pain. Now, as an observer, it made her nauseous and a little faint.

"There will be something in the pack I give you," Bindes said. "She should have stitches to minimize the scarring. But she will heal."

"I can sew her up," Rick said. "We have more coag powder, but no thread or needles."

"It will be too late to suture the wound by the time Sofie gets back. Use the surgical tape to hold the edges of the skin together. The incision didn't cut an artery, so the bleeding will stop completely soon. Clean the wound, tape it and use the coag powder. Not so much of it. I'll send a full professional medical kit and a pack of shots with a hypo to speed her healing."

There was a moment of silence before Bindes said, "You can look now."

Sofie blushed but turned back to him. "How long will she be out?"

"Let her sleep as much as you can. Six hours rest minimum before she's more alert. No heavy action for a full day if possible." He looked at the scan again and groaned. "But you don't have that much time, right? So, when she wakes, she'll need another four hours recovery before you let her push herself. You should know, blood loss is going to make her body weak and her mind slow. You might not be able to rely on her reasoning for a bit."

They needed someone to stay in the room, so Amanda could be their eyes until she was ready to go out.

"Okay, so I'm fine. Amanda will be fine. Good. Get the stuff together for me to take back and I'm gone right after you tell me what you know about who's running the situation on the Mallet right now."

He pulled a medical kit from a drawer and opened it. Inside were all the usual supplies, along with a few Sofie didn't recognize. And a paper book — rare and expensive, but also not at risk of being shut down if the network was damaged.

"You have people on the streets," Bindes said. "They should be able to find the leaders pretty fast."

"You know everything that goes on around here," Sofie said. "I can't stop this without information."

Yes, Haadiya's people should have come up with something by now, but they were starting from scratch. Bindes wasn't. He knew people at every level, from his meds supplier to the most desperate dark street resident.

"If I knew for sure, I would have reported them. I know how this situation is likely to end."

"I promise I won't railroad anyone. Whoever you suspect will do. You have good instincts."

He closed the lid of the medical kit after adding a handful of blister packs to the contents. He handed it to her and said, "The meds will help her regain her strength, but there will be a cost in the future. Make sure she's watched."

"If there's a future." Sofie stood and stepped a little closer to Bindes. "I'll keep your name out of it, but I need someone with answers."

He shook his head and closed his eyes in what Sofie hoped was resignation.

"It's the only way," she said.

"The man's name is Virgil Ten. I don't know where he is, but he is involved somehow."

Sofie thanked him and opened the office door.

A quick check of her wrist comm showed clear streets from the Open Pit to the case room. A newsfeed reported that the rioters had been quelled.

For now.

27

Rick took the medical kit from Sofie as she walked through the door. Everyone was back from their errands. Good, no need to worry anyone else was bleeding to death in the middle of a riot.

"I have a name," Sofie said. "Anyone else have luck?" She looked directly at Haadiya. He was supposed to be their information conduit, and so far he'd been useless. Well, the tokens were a life saver, but only if they needed passage.

Haadiya shook his head. "It seems my spies are being shut out. I suggest we have them bring your lead to us rather than hope for more." He sat beside Nhu at the desk.

Amanda would have already told Sofie if she found anything out at the bullpen. Rick wouldn't have waited to tell her if he had a name. Nhu was with Rick the entire time, and they seemed to be of limited use in generating information.

She needed to trust Haadiya, but she couldn't stop questioning his every action and word. Time to deal with that problem. "Why did you give us the tokens if your people all know you want us to be helped?" The question had bothered her since the first guard on the dark streets dismissed the token.

Haadiya smiled as though she'd asked a particularly clever question. It pissed Sofie off, but she chose not to react.

"You needed to be sure of my promise," he said. "Would you have believed me so easily if I simply stated that you could draw on my resources?"

A good point, but not enough. "So, if we leave them here, it won't matter?" If he was using the tokens as a tracking device, or recording their conversations, he'd object.

"If you feel better without them," he said. "Perhaps it's wiser to continue to carry them. If you should ask for help in the middle of a... heated situation, shall we call it? The token may speed up the correct response."

This was the problem with him. Never giving Sofie enough to decide whether or not she could trust him. "Okay. We'll keep using them," she said. "Have your spies reported anything useful? Even without a name, we need to know if someone is deciding where the riots break out. Or when."

"I have instructed my best people to find a way to join the mob, and the others are retreating to the safety of the dark streets." He glanced at the wall of screens. "Can you spare one of these to hold the messages they send me?"

"Provide me access, and I'll take care of it," Nhu said. "Now that Amanda is out of commission, I will become the technology expert."

So, the two people she trusted the least were in charge of communications and situation reports. Great. At least she trusted Rick to help her on the streets.

"I can also have this person brought to us," Haadiya offered. "Or a separate location if that is preferred."

"What condition will he arrive in?" Sofie asked.

"The same condition they find him in," Haadiya said. "I assume if you need to beat answers from him, you would like to ask the questions first?"

Again, he wanted her to trust his word, or his control over the people he used. This man who'd lived a double life from birth; one his family had hidden for generations. Expert liars who protected the most degenerate of the Mallet criminal element.

If she had a choice, Sofie would kick him out of the team. But if she only worked with people she could prove were trustworthy, she'd be alone. Nhu was as bad as Haadiya. Amanda was so ambitious she might do anything for promotion. Rick? He hadn't turned on her yet, but that was no guarantee.

Years of fear about being caught with the Fades weighed her down. A little voice in the back of her mind warned her about offending Executives every time she had to speak to Nhu or Haadiya. Maybe this was not about whether these people could be trusted, but more about Sofie needing to learn to be trusting.

"Have them bring him here," she said, deciding to put aside her concerns until someone proved they didn't deserve her trust. "No damage. If he's been beaten before they find him, they need to take images. They don't question him. If taking him will cause violence, they need to find a way to avoid it."

"My people do have subtlety, Sofie. The name?"

"Virgil Ten. I don't know anything else."

Haadiya typed instructions on his wrist comm. Sofie saw the words appear on the center screen *Find Virgil Ten. Bring him to my location unharmed. Advise when you are approaching. No drama.*

"See? Everything is out in the open." Haadiya stood. "Stim-juice, anyone?"

Sofie asked for Rellian blufroot, told herself that being served by an Executive was not a sign of equality, and turned to Rick, who was wrapping Amanda in a blanket. "How is she?"

"All bound up. She said she feels better. The healing meds seemed to relax her, and her skin is looking healthier. Your doctor said she's to rest for as long as we can force her to. No exertion for ten hours."

"Pretty much what he said to me. With luck, it will all be over by then. One way or another. Did you hear what we were talking about?"

"Yeah. You and me in the interrogation?"

"I need Nhu and Haadiya separated from it," she said. "What does the unit next door look like?"

"Bare, like the other ones Llewelyn set up. I can pull in a couple of chairs. No tables available."

"When we're done, someone needs to take him to one of the cells."

"Haadiya's people?"

She grunted a laugh. "I'm trying to trust him, but we'll see."

"We'll figure something out." Rick touched Amanda's cheek. She didn't respond. "She's safe here for now."

28

The screen showing the communication between Haadiya and the people searching for Virgil Ten moved too fast for Sofie to keep track of the individual messages. Along with what seemed to be a running commentary on the street, Nhu added her research on the man to help set up the capture.

"Got him," Haadiya announced an hour after the search began, a grin on his face making him look younger. "This is exciting. If you can get more names, I'm happy to direct the search."

"It's not a game. I want to see his face now," Sofie said.

Haadiya sent two messages. One to stop the constant reports from people still looking for Virgil Ten and the other to take and transmit a photo.

The man was around Sofie's height, so half a head shorter than most men on the Mallet. His hair was dull gray and his skin was only a few shades darker, where it wasn't livid with bruising. He stood between two tall dark streets thugs. Neither was touching him, but he held his right arm in his left like it was damaged.

"I said no violence." Sofie snapped the words to Haadiya.

"I don't think they did it," Haadiya said.

"Why?" Sofie glanced at Rick and then at the medical kit.

"Two reasons. They will be punished if they disobey me, and my people *don't* disobey me."

"We'll see what he tells us," Sofie said, trying to keep an open mind. If Haadiya was so confident, her suspicion might be completely wrong. "How long before they drop him off?"

"Ten minutes." Haadiya closed the message thread, and the screen went blank.

"Nhu, what did you find on Virgil Ten?" Sofie asked. "We need something to use as leverage to get him to talk."

"He is a supervisor in Manufacturing. No family." Nhu flicked the data onto a screen. "Had the job for ten years. He seems to have performed well. I see no complaints to worry about. There are a few brawls, but he was not charged."

A man with few ties. So, the mess we're dealing with is probably for selfish reasons. "Okay, Rick, I'll start with sympathy and trying to understand who beat him up and why. You go in when he's weak."

"I should be in the room," Haadiya said. "I am intimidating."

"If he's organizing the riots, he's not going to be intimidated by an Executive," Sofie said.

"You haven't seen me play the role fully," Haadiya said.

"There's nothing in his record about insubordination," Nhu said. "He may indeed be prone to obey superiors."

Then he should be willing to be honest with a cop.

"If he needs to be intimidated, Rick is good at doing that just standing in a corner." She didn't want Haadiya in the room with her. Interrogation required teamwork, and he wasn't trained to play the game. Intimidation only worked if the subject felt it. She needed more information on Virgil Ten to even guess if it would work.

"I agree with Haadiya," Rick said.

Why did everyone have to argue with her? Perhaps the 'we're all equals' deal was too broad. "Why? You and I are a good team."

Rick looked up at the ceiling as if the right words were printed there. "Don't get me wrong. I know we can do it. I wouldn't normally agree to have a civilian in the room because they have no clue about the game. No offense, Haadiya."

"Not just a civilian," Haadiya said. "I do have some experience extracting information from reluctant people."

"That's why I don't want you there," Sofie said. "You are too ready to cross some lines I don't want crossed."

"You would sacrifice the Mallet's future because you don't want this man to feel bad about himself?" Haadiya asked.

"Another reason I want Rick in the room," Sofie said. "He understands the way things work. And, no, of course I don't care if he feels shame, but if we must cross the line, I don't want it to be the first thing we do."

"Sofie, you've got a few minutes to give him the rules," Rick said. "I should go looking in the Temporaries. We need to know what's happening there. If anyone else is paying to be smuggled out, or if there's anyone left in the section, or, I don't know, something."

Sofie had been so intent on the interrogation, she'd lost focus on the situation outside. Right now, they were all acting like the next riot was going to explode any moment. But Rick had a point. If the outgoing Temporaries were empty, it meant something. If some other group was trying to get out, it meant something. And she was supposed to be trusting people. Maybe Rick could find a clue there to explain why Torque was sure he'd be back.

"Go now," she said to Rick. "I'll deal with Virgil's injuries. Haadiya, if you're going to be the lurking menace in the room, he needs to know you're the boss of the dark streets."

He raised an eyebrow but must have decided not to fight her. "I suppose the truth is out now. I'll deal with it when we survive the current mess. Do you want him certain it's me? Or shall we have him worried about which of us is the boss?"

"I like the idea of him wondering if it's me," she said with a smile.

"Then I will have his escorts inform him that he will be joining their boss."

Sofie looked for Rick, but he'd already slipped out.

"Let me give you a fast rundown on how an interrogation works when it's not a criminal mastermind running the show."

29

"But wouldn't it be a better idea to get him worried about how far we'll go?" Haadiya asked when Sofie finished telling him the plan.

"It's a tactic," she agreed. "We don't threaten torture, ever. He should be worried about getting charged for a more serious crime or taking the fall for everything, not getting electric shocks to his genitals."

Now she understood how he led the dark streets. If everyone who lived there was constantly afraid of the kind of punishment he'd hand out, then they'd do his bidding.

"You are not set up for torture," Haadiya said. "I can ask someone to bring a few instruments if it gets that far. The threat of pain would get him talking faster."

Or he would shut down completely. Or he would lie and hope to live beyond us finding the truth.

"Keep it for if I decide we need it later," Sofie said, hoping normal techniques would get the man to talk.

"Three people approaching the door," Nhu said.

Haadiya checked the screen. "Yes, this is who we are expecting."

Sofie opened the connecting door to the empty unit, then noticed Rick must have dragged the bed pads out. The bunk frames were locked against the wall. The man wouldn't be able to make anything into a weapon. She nodded to Haadiya.

He thanked his men and assured them he was safe, then pulled a blindfolded prisoner through to the space, giving him a little push to make him stumble.

A little roughness was fine with Sofie, and the blindfold had been a great idea. She would ask for it next time, if they got another lead. It meant Virgil had no idea where he was, or who else was in the room.

"You can take off the blindfold," Sofie said.

"I am an Executive. I do not stoop to menial tasks," Haadiya said with his usual demeaning tone. It wasn't exactly what she'd told him to do, but the result was the same. Virgil knew his rank but didn't know for sure he was the boss of the dark streets.

Sofie reached for the strip of fabric. "I'll look at your wounds before we start. There's a chair behind you."

Virgil blinked at the light, which Sofie had set at full brightness to put him off kilter. She nodded to the chair and waited until the man sat. Haadiya leaned against the wall behind their prisoner.

"He should tell us what he knows before you tend to him," Haadiya said. "Traitors don't deserve to use critical supplies."

"It's only a few pills and bandages," Sofie said. Haadiya was handling his half of the plan well.

"I'm not a traitor," Virgil said. "I'm looking out for the exploited workers."

Sofie dabbed at the blood on his lip, and he winced. She

handed him two pills. "No major damage. Take these, they'll reduce the pain."

Virgil looked around. "I need water. Can't swallow these dry."

"Then you will feel all the pain," Haadiya said. The way he stressed the word 'all' made it clear he wasn't talking about his current injuries.

"Sorry, he's right. I can't leave you alone with him," Sofie said. Let Virgil imagine what would happen if she left. "We have a few questions."

Virgil glanced at the pills and then tucked them in a pocket. "I'm not telling you anything."

Sofie looked at Haadiya and gave her head a small shake as though to say, *not yet*. Virgil might think she was the boss of the dark streets, but if he thought she was protecting him, it would help too.

"I'll ask them anyway," she said, standing from her crouch. "I don't think anyone wants this situation to escalate."

"What situation?" Virgil asked.

"The riots." Sofie put some surprise in her voice. "If it gets worse, we're all dead."

"Why do you think I know anything about it?"

Haadiya stepped into Virgil's line of sight. "Do you think we're pulling in random people? Someone gave us your name. Someone who might just want to shift blame away from themselves. Keep quiet and it will work."

Sofie glared at Haadiya, finding she enjoyed playing the role of defender.

"Who? No one but the leaders have our identities."

"So you *are* one of the leaders," Sofie said. "Good. Now we know you have the answers we need. Just make it easy on yourself."

"Who?" Virgil asked again.

"I can't tell you," Sofie said.

"You give us some names and maybe we'll confirm who gave us you as a scapegoat," Haadiya said.

Virgil looked down at his lap. Sofie could see his lips moving but it wasn't names. If he was trying to talk himself out of helping, he needed a push. Not torture, but something strong.

"If you don't help us, then when everything settles down, you will be spaced," Sofie said, then touched his knee to break his concentration on his inner thoughts. "You ever seen a live body sent out?"

"I have," Haadiya said. "It is quite a lesson in biology. Every single person screams. Like we can hear them through the station walls. And then ice crystals form on their skin. I particularly like the way it shatters the eyes. Of course, if they exploded it would be more exciting, but that doesn't happen unless some debris slams through them."

"You're sick," Virgil said.

Haadiya stepped closer and leaned in. Sofie expected him to whisper so that she wouldn't hear the threat. He spoke in a normal voice; no anger, just flat. "You do not say that sort of thing to an Executive without repercussions."

"We talked about this," Sofie said.

Haadiya didn't respond. He kept talking. "If you are of no use, perhaps we can arrange for you to take a one-way trip through an airlock now."

Virgil pulled away, then grabbed his ribs and winced. "The days of you higher castes treating us this way are over. Let me go."

Haadiya smiled, reminding Sofie of a raptor she'd seen on a vid from C'koo. She expected him to sniff and flick out his tongue for a taste. "Not yet, Virgil. Maybe never."

"Ask me the fucking questions and get this asshole away from me."

Sofie told Haadiya to back off. He sighed but moved back to the corner.

"Who is directing this action?" Sofie asked.

"I don't know."

Haadiya moved his feet to make a noise and Virgil flinched.

"I really don't know. We get messages to go to a meeting space. I don't recognize the voice when it talks, and it's only audio."

Not helpful, but that wasn't Virgil's fault. Sofie believed he was telling the truth as he knew it.

"Who are the other organizers?"

"I don't know, we never see each other. We're all kind of behind screens, like the same unit but partitioned off." Virgil heard Haadiya move again. Sofie saw the panic in his eyes as he searched for something to appease the monster. "Look. I know when the next meeting is. I have my comm. I'll give you the codes."

30

Virgil either didn't know the names of his colleagues, or Haadiya's threats were not enough for him to give them up. Some people were like that — loyal and stupid.

"He had his pad on him. It's unlocked," Sofie said, handing it to Nhu. "Can you try to find the other people getting the messages? And a physical location on anyone you find?"

Nhu flipped the pad around and opened it. "If this contact is smart enough, nothing will be traceable. Better to wait for the next invitation. I can trace an active call to the source and find the other participants."

Sofie glanced over at Amanda. Still asleep, but that was probably the best thing for her. She wasn't sure of Nhu's skills, but Amanda had displayed her magic level of tech manipulation many times in the past.

"Do your best," she said. "I'm letting Virgil stew for a bit. I'll go back in alone and try another approach. He might not know the other names for sure, but I'm confident he has a guess."

"Where will he go when you are done with him?" Nhu asked. "That room was supposed to be our sleeping quarters."

"I doubt we will be sleeping until this is over, but we could dispose of him," Haadiya said. He turned on the stim-juice machine before reaching down and checking Amanda. "I mean, he's going to be dead soon anyway, why inconvenience ourselves?"

Yes, one way or another, Virgil would die. Either the Mallet would explode and he'd die with everyone else, or Sofie and her team would stop the madness and he'd be found guilty and condemned to death. She wasn't ready to take on the role of executioner yet. And it was too far to the closest airlock anyway.

"We'll keep him here for now. There's a camera in there; is it working?"

Nhu stopped playing with Virgil's pad and checked their own. "Yes. So, not only do you expect me to give up my privacy, but I'm also observing him so he doesn't hurt himself?"

Unless he flipped the chair and impaled himself, there was no way to do even a little damage. "I need to see when he's ready for round two," she said. "When he realizes he might have a chance to save himself if he shifts the blame around."

"Why did you ask for more units if you didn't intend to use them?" Nhu snapped as they put the camera feed onto another screen.

"Will we be able to watch other prisoners?" The units would work well for a jail, but prisoners needed to be watched. If something went wrong, like a mob breaking in, the sooner they knew the better.

Nhu searched their pad again. Sofie wondered just how many places they could access.

"Three of them," Nhu said. "Do you want to choose which screen I place them on? What information we won't have access to in order to watch blank screens?"

Nhu's interpretation of working as equals seemed to be sullen compliance. Better than fighting for control over every little decision, but not much.

"None right now," Sofie said. "I'm sure when we have people inside the rooms, you will be able to split one screen for those cameras."

She felt petty responding in the same tone to Nhu, but she didn't have the energy to keep being sweet to someone who didn't respond in kind.

Nhu nodded and returned to Virgil's pad. "When will Amanda be able to take on a share of this work? I did not come here to be the only person capable of working the technology."

"She will require at least three more hours of sleep, more if she can manage it," Haadiya said. "Her pressure is normal, her heart is beating more regularly, and she has no fever. But she was very close to death by the time we were able to treat her. I suggest you plan on working solo for quite some time."

Sofie turned away to hide the smile his tone brought to her face. No matter how often she told herself Nhu was supposed to accept her as an equal, she would never be able to speak so plainly to them.

"I would prefer fewer interruptions," Nhu said. "Perhaps you can move to the other side of the unit. I will inform you if your prisoner changes attitude."

So that was them told off. Sofie poured a stim-juice,

added flavor, and joined Haadiya in what had been the second unit.

"It would be better if the building team had simply made a connecting door between these units, like they did for the one Virgil now inhabits, rather than removing the wall," Haadiya said. "Nhu is correct that we all need privacy."

"When we get what we need from Virgil, we'll move him to one of the other units," Sofie said. "But not yet. I think he has more to tell us."

"I will task my spies with finding his friends. Perhaps this mystery person is using them. I wonder how someone found the right people to incite such stupid violence."

"I'm not sure that's the right question. Who wouldn't be willing to change things? If we find them, I don't want these friends to come in beaten up," Sofie said.

"He's crying," Nhu called.

"Don't come in," Sofie said to Haadiya. "You can watch on the monitor."

He shifted position to be able to see the screen and stay as far away from Nhu as possible.

Sofie opened the door to Virgil's cell. He looked up and she saw he was ready to tell her anything he could think of if it meant he had a chance to live. "If I tell you my guesses, will you help me get a deal?"

She had no power to do it, and she suspected no one involved would even survive to get a trial, but Virgil didn't know that.

"I'll do what I can. Right now, you are the only one we have, so you get the best chance at a deal."

"I recognized the voices."

"Okay, tell me who they are."

"One is a supervisor in Maintenance, and the other is a bistro owner," he said. "Kaylee Elton and Zack Spinner."

"Your friends?"

"Not really. I worked with Kaylee a couple of times a year ago. I go to Zack's every day for stim-juice or lunch." He confirmed they'd be at the meeting place coordinates he'd already given her.

Sofie left the room without another word. Virgil wasn't finished sharing his information, but she had enough to take action. The rest could wait.

31

"I'm heading out," Sofie said. She picked up her stunner and shoved it in her holster.

"Who's going with you?" Nhu asked. "It's too dangerous for you to go alone."

Rick is out there by himself.

"Haadiya can play doctor to Amanda, and I trust you to keep him from tormenting our prisoner — or worse. I'll be alert."

"Take Haadiya," Nhu said. "Amanda is sleeping. I think I can manage to watch her."

As the boss of the dark streets, Haadiya would know how to keep them safe. But Sofie didn't trust him knowing where these people could be found, no matter how much he seemed to have dropped the caste behavior. "I don't need a bodyguard."

"I find myself agreeing with Nhu," Haadiya said. "If I'm with you, then the prisoner is safe. Although I assure you, I had no plans to deal with him."

"Then you can be the doctor if Amanda wakes up. She won't lie still willingly. I'll be fine."

"How long do you intend to stay out?" Nhu asked. "And where are you going?"

"Why?" Nhu would observe her on the tracker, Haadiya too.

"If you insist on going alone, I want to know where to send help if needed."

This was the only lead they had, but more than that, it could turn out to be what they needed to stop whoever was feeding the rage of the protesters. Taking the leaders off the streets gave them time. Whoever was driving this would need to find new idiots to use. If telling Nhu would stop the argument, she would override her concerns and do it.

"Where is Rick?" she asked. "Maybe he can join me."

Nhu glanced at the screen. "Deep in the outgoing Temporaries."

"Fine. I'm going to find the other two leaders. Virgil gave me the location and names. I have their images on my comm."

"You can't bring in two people on your own," Haadiya said. "I understand you don't trust my lieutenants to do it, but Nhu is right. I will come with you."

Sofie couldn't explain the instinct to leave him in the case room. Every point Nhu made to get her to take Haadiya with her was valid. She couldn't bring in both of the suspects, so she was risking losing one of the leaders and alerting the other. Neither location was near one of the jail units they had. Even if they were, how was she going to drag the person across a volatile section without triggering the very thing she was desperate to stop?

"Grab a stunner," she said to him. "They're all charged."

"No need." Haadiya flicked his coat open to show two stunners at his hips. "And I think we need to consider using my lieutenants. We find the culprit and then we hand them over for transport."

"And find them bloody and bruised when we go to interrogate them?"

He gave her an indulgent smile. "You will see the original state of these people. My people will not damage them any further."

She turned to Nhu. "When Rick gets back, update him, then let us know."

Something flashed across their face. Annoyance at Sofie's tone, or at the words? "Of course, I take my coordination duties seriously."

"Let's get this done before we're trapped," Sofie said.

"Rick is nearby," Nhu said. "He must have news if he got here so fast. Perhaps you should wait?"

"How long?" she asked.

"The streets are clear, a few minutes."

It could be a mistake. Waiting for Rick might make the difference between catching and missing her targets. But if he had vital information that changed their tactics, she couldn't afford to miss it.

"Okay, we'll wait," she said, hoping it wasn't a mistake. "Maybe he has news that will change things."

And I can take him instead of Haadiya.

32

Sofie was getting antsy by the time Rick stepped through the door. Only three minutes after Nhu's announcement, but still time for her to question her decision to wait again.

"They're gone," he said. "The entire population of the Temporaries. That Ulindia security company is blocking anyone without authority from entering. I'm assuming it's the same up front."

Not a surprise, but why were the Elite Families paying for the outside help?

"Did they try to stop you?" Sofie asked.

"No, but on my way out, I was told to keep my attention on the Mallet proper and not worry about the client areas. Since when has any part of the Mallet been in the control of clients?"

"Since the first contract was signed, and it's not just the Temporaries," Nhu said. "Another thing the Elites suppressed."

"So, what does it mean?" Sofie asked. "The Elites think

they can come back? The clients are just covering the possibility we'll quell the violence?"

"We do need to find answers to your questions, Sofie," Haadiya said. "But first, we should ensure the Mallet survives, yes?"

The answers might just make the difference between dying as the station collapses, or saving it. "Maybe these two leads will help us get there," she said. Then she brought Rick up to date.

"You want me to come?" he asked.

"Yes," she said, surprised at his question. "Haadiya and Nhu can search records and documents to find the reasons why. Our job is to save the Mallet."

"I know, but we can't separate it. The reason someone decided now was the time to cause an insurrection might lead to our way to save everyone." Rick rubbed his eyes. "I guess I need some rest soon. I forgot to say we're outgunned by the Ulindia guys, and if the rioters get their hands on some of their weapons, we won't have a chance."

Another thing she should have thought about. Strategy wasn't ever going to be her strength. "Okay, so we need to get some heavier armaments. Shock prods? Lethal stunners?"

Rick nodded. "I can go to the bullpen and get them. Give Llewelyn a heads up if he doesn't already know."

"He was clear that we were on our own," Sofie said. "Even if he talks to you, there's no guarantee he can spare weapons."

The cops had their job to do, and Llewelyn needed to focus on that. He'd put the task force together for a reason.

"I may be of assistance," Haadiya said. "The weapons you need may have found their way into the dark streets. Just for emergencies like this, of course."

Fuck. Was everyone ready for rebellion except the people who were supposed to prevent it?

"Can you bring us some of your hypothetical stock?" she asked. "I have to go after the two people Virgil gave up."

"I wouldn't know what you need," Haadiya said. "I have a proposal."

"What?"

"You and I continue with the original plan. I arrange for Rick to meet my armorer and he can choose whatever you need from our supplies."

Rick would know what to bring, but so would she. Too many choices. She needed to focus on the immediate options. Trying to solve the entire problem at once was foolish. They had two tasks — well, three. Nhu could take care of the research, and Sofie believed they wouldn't actually harm Virgil. Amanda wouldn't wake for a couple of hours. That left two actions to complete. Get the leaders in custody to disrupt the plans for the Mallet's future, whatever they were, and make sure they were equipped to face resistance. There really was only one answer.

"Haadiya and I will go for the two leaders. We'll use his people to transport them to the spare units for questioning. Rick, go get us the weapons we need."

"Give me the location of your armory," Rick said.

"Oh, I think we'll keep that secret," Haadiya said. "Nhu, please disconnect your tracker on Rick for one hour." He typed something into his pad. "One of my lieutenants will meet you at the Open Pit. Once inside the streets, you will be blindfolded until you arrive at the armory to do your shopping."

As much as she wanted to say no, Sofie understood everyone had secrets to keep. "And your people are not to be brought back here," she said. "If Rick needs to make multiple trips to bring the equipment back, he'll have to do it."

"No need," Haadiya said. "My supplies include transports. There will be a dolly or a flat bed. Now, we should go."

"How are the streets, Nhu?" Sofie asked.

"Clear to the Open Pit," they answered. "Since I don't know your destination, I cannot provide further information."

They were pissed at her. Sofie smiled. In normal circumstances it would be a huge mistake; today, it was just the way things went.

"Any hot spots?" she asked.

"Stay away from your bullpen. Be alert. If I am able to keep your trackers on, I can advise you as you go."

"That will work." Sofie nodded to Haadiya. "Let's go."

33

"If they all go to private terminals for instructions, someone on the Mallet must be controlling the location," Haadiya said.

Sofie didn't want to chat. The location for the meeting was at the edge of Nhu's suggested safe zone. The streets might be clear where they were, but she could hear raised voices nearby. "Why?"

"They need to make sure the location is available, and out of the way of any planned riots. Unless you lived here, you couldn't guarantee either of those things."

"Just pay attention. We don't want to end up like Amanda." She sped up her pace. The meeting was in thirty minutes, according to Virgil. Under normal circumstances, it wouldn't be a problem. Now, if she had to detour halfway across the Mallet to get there, it could mean she'd miss the chance to catch the two people.

"My people are clearing the way," Haadiya said. "Nothing violent, I assure you. We may be criminals, but we understand how violence just creates more violence when a crowd is involved."

She paused at a cross street and looked down it. At the end, a figure in a dark cloak stood facing her. In his or her hands, she could see stunners. Not the usual police issue; these were larger and decorated with bright paint. A sample of the weapons Rick would be collecting, maybe.

"I hope you're right and your people have the discipline to hold back when challenged."

"You are very welcome," Haadiya said, as though she'd thanked him. "What is the plan when we arrive?"

"If someone on the station is passing on messages, we need to know," she answered. "If we can't apprehend the two people before they go in, I'll pretend to be there as Virgil's replacement. We get what we need from the conversation and then we take the other two into custody." There was a danger no one would believe that she'd taken over from Virgil. And if Virgil's original story about screened off partitions wasn't a lie, she'd have an easier time.

"You'll need something to cover the cop in you," Haadiya said. He tapped his wrist comm. "We'll have a change of clothes, and some pattern disruption bands you can put on your face."

Pattern disruption bands were to confuse the surveillance drones, but Sofie had been fooled by them in person before. Haadiya was turning out to be a good partner, but she couldn't quite let go of the lifetime of suspicion of the higher castes, or the urge to arrest a criminal. "How did you manage to be a liaison to the Sato Second and run the dark streets without anyone knowing?"

"My lieutenants knew," he said. "But outside the dark streets, people tend to accept you as you present yourself. As an Executive, no one lower would dare even speculate. My peers had no reason to think I lived a double life, and the Elites only see us as tools."

I should have thought about it before I asked. Everyone on the Mallet was a tool to the Elites. Maybe this current situation was being driven by someone who saw the Elites that way. "I wonder, how many other people in your caste had separate identities?"

Haadiya checked his wrist comm. "Your disguise is ready, and my people are in place. As to your question, we'll never know the extent of it, but don't you think this all has the smell of a high caste plot? My Executive colleagues are possibly trying to create a leadership void, and then fill it."

"It could only be an Executive, right?" She slowed as a figure stepped into the path and beckoned.

Haadiya walked beside her to join his lieutenant. "Or an Elite who wants more power. They have a hierarchy, as you are quite aware. Why do you think no one clamored for Tran Gilbride to be found?"

The man had been an Elite, and was now dead. But only six people on the Mallet knew that. Sofie, Rick, Amanda, Nhu, and Haadiya were the ones who agreed to blame the man. The other person who knew, a Maintenance supervisor named Mitch, kept quiet because it was the only way he wouldn't be charged with the murder — even though he was innocent. "I assumed it was because people believed he got off the Mallet. Out of our jurisdiction."

"He was barely hanging on to his status," Haadiya said. "Here we are." He thanked the lieutenant and sent him on his way. "Do you need privacy to change clothes?"

The gray coverall was two sizes bigger than Sofie needed. "I'll just put it on over what I'm wearing." She noticed the pockets were cut out. The garment looked whole at a glance, but if she arranged the belt correctly, her stunners were in reach through the slits. "Nice tailoring."

"My people are not stupid, Sofie." He picked up a package and opened it. "Let me place the bands."

Sofie closed her eyes and mouth. She breathed shallowly to give Haadiya as steady a canvas as possible. The bands needed to be completely flat on her skin. A wrinkle would result in the whole piece sliding off.

"Perhaps when this is all done, we can discuss giving some of my more stable residents a second chance?" He ran his finger along the band that crossed her cheeks and nose.

Sofie fought to stay still at this touch. This was a big step past her personal trust level.

Another band crossed her forehead, and then two oval patches pressed into her chin and throat.

"Done. Just count to ten before you move to let it set."

She counted slowly and then opened her eyes to see Haadiya's pad facing her, the camera turned to the front, acting as a mirror. For a moment, Sofie didn't recognize herself.

"This isn't the standard patch," she said. "Is there anything you can't get?"

"I'm an Executive, Sofie. I get what I want." He turned the pad off and dropped it into a pocket.

"What you said about second chances, do you really think it's possible?" Sofie wasn't sure why she asked the question.

"Whatever the outcome of this current strife, the Mallet will be different. Are you ready?"

She nodded and checked her weapons one more time.

34

Inside, the small unit looked exactly like Virgil described it. A table stood in the center, and privacy screens running from floor to ceiling divided it into four sections, each with a door behind the chair. The screens were set to allow only a shadow of what was there. The fourth section didn't have a chair, just a screen.

She could see outlines of three chairs, so no one else had arrived. Haadiya's guards would be waiting to warn her that others were approaching. The meeting would go ahead. She let the breath out that she'd been holding in anticipation of problems.

Sofie sent a message to Haadiya describing what she saw. *Can you trace any connections to this unit? Maybe we'll find the mysterious contact's location.*

Good idea.

Nothing else came through. Sofie sat and waited. The meeting was due to start in three minutes.

The privacy screens meant no one would know Virgil wasn't in the room. Of course, unless they knew he was under arrest. Or they forced her to speak. If she could,

Sofie wanted the others to think Virgil was still in play. If forced to speak, she'd tell them he'd been arrested, and hope they'd accept her as his replacement. She didn't imagine there was a lot of chatting at these meetings. So it was possible she'd succeed in keeping Virgil's arrest quiet.

The screen flickered and a bright blob appeared in the center.

She was still alone.

"Our time is almost here." The voice came from the screen. It was heavily enhanced. Each word in a different voice, mechanical, soft, harsh, male, female, androgynous.

"When the Mallet is free, you will stand down. Now is not the time to pause action. Now is the time to accelerate the discord."

Clearly the contact had no idea if anyone was listening and didn't care, which was worrying. If the voice was directing the action to an empty room, how would her plan succeed?

Sofie didn't speak. Haadiya's trace was the only thing they'd get out of this lead. That, and learning about the plan for the Mallet. If the person behind the screen didn't know she was here, she wasn't planning to let them know.

"You want peace now. We understand. The Elite families have deserted their posts. A better future is coming. But the work toward change must continue."

A better future? Was that all it took for people to risk everything? And who on the Mallet was naive enough to believe things would change for the better? Or that better meant the same thing to them as it did to the people behind the unrest?

"You know the next steps. You must push harder to reach the goal."

So much for gathering intel on the details of the plan. Or even a hint about who was truly running the show.

The screen flickered for a moment. Was this meeting over?

"You will be rewarded. Your actions are building a more equal Mallet. Remember, individuals will fall; regret their deaths, but celebrate their sacrifice for the people who survive."

The screen went dark. So, another greater good argument. The tactic was as old as humanity. Sofie waited a moment in case the message wasn't finished. But the screen stayed blank.

She slipped outside and looked for Haadiya. He was sitting at a stim-juice bar across the way. It was open, which made her suspicious. Most businesses kept their shutters down these days.

"Rellian blufroot?" he asked, passing her a large drink.

"How did you make the owner open up?" She took a sip.

"It's one of mine," he said, as if she knew he owned businesses outside the dark streets. "I fund many of these. If we get a chance to be legitimate, we take it. We need income that isn't hidden."

If he was this far along, his plan to make the dark streets an accepted part of the Mallet was not new. It didn't matter. Sofie would not be asked her opinion on the decision. "Did you get a trace?"

"Oh, yes. Many. This contact is bouncing their signal all around the Mallet. The only place that didn't get a hit on the signal was the Temporaries. Both ends."

"And what happened to the other two leaders?" It occurred to her that Haadiya's guards had taken them before they entered the unit.

"I suggest you let my people search for them." He nodded across the way. "No one came near."

Dead? Or warned?

"You think the contact knows we have Virgil?"

"To be perfectly honest, perhaps for the first time in my life, I don't even have a guess. This person is not acting in a sane manner from our point of view. They have a plan, yes?"

Sofie nodded and then told him what happened in the unit. "I don't have the authority to deputize your people."

Haadiya grinned. "Oh, Sofie, are you lying to me, or have you forgotten?"

For a moment she couldn't think what he meant. Then Llewelyn's words came to her. "I have all kinds of authority. And no details about what I can't do. And Nhu was assigned to us so they could give us cover when it's over."

"For anyone else on the Mallet, that would have been a license to steal and get rid of rivals. But your team is unusually dedicated to justice."

"Not all of us," Sofie said.

"I can't speak for Nhu, but I am here for a form of justice."

"Can I trust your people not to take advantage of being deputized?"

"No. But you can trust me." He tapped a message into his wrist comm. "Where next?"

Sofie was saved from saying she had no clue when her comm chimed. "Amanda is awake."

35

"How are you feeling?" Sofie asked. Amanda should still be sleeping, but if she was well enough to work, Sofie wouldn't turn down her help. After all, she'd come back to work before the doctor recommended and she was fine.

"Used up," Amanda said. "I'm fine to work at a screen. Can you come back?"

Every time the investigation led them to the streets, something drew them back to the case room. If there was even a tiny lead, Sofie would have reason to stay out, but she didn't have a legitimate clue. Maybe she didn't need an excuse. "What's going on?"

Amanda glanced over her shoulder, then back. "Nhu. They want me to get this Virgil guy to another location. I can't go back to the streets yet, Sofie."

That was hard for her to admit.

"I thought we settled it." Why did Nhu keep pushing on this issue? The man was safer in the unit with them. Transporting him to one of the empty units was dangerous. He could escape. Whatever happened to the other two leaders might be waiting for him on the streets. A riot could overwhelm whoever played escort. And maybe the most important thing, he was their only access to information. He'd kept things back before, so maybe he still had tidbits to offer.

"I guess not," Amanda said. "He's locked in that unit, so I don't know why they are in such a fit about it. If you can't come, do you know where Rick is? Or Haadiya?"

"Didn't Nhu bring you up to date?" Sofie flicked a glance at Haadiya, who was listening to the conversation. He shrugged.

"No. They were on a comm call when I came around. What did I miss?"

"Not a lot, as it turns out. Rick is off to get us heavier weapons from the dark streets. Haadiya is with me. We heard the message from the contact, but it didn't get us any closer to solving the case. I guess we're coming in, so I'll give you the details when we get there."

"Can I do anything while I wait?" Amanda asked. "I can be helpful even if I'm stuck here."

Sofie gave her the names of the two other leaders. "Can you try to locate them? Haadiya's guys will bring them in, but if we help, maybe we can speed it up?"

She wasn't going to give Amanda the content of the video message on an open line.

"Okay, how long before you get here?"

"Depends on whether we run into a riot or a protest," Sofie said. "It seems quiet here. You have anything on the rest of the station?" She couldn't bring herself to trust the public screens. They may be free of the hack, but someone could be suppressing the real feeds in an attempt to slow down the violence. It wouldn't work, but only a few people knew about the concerted effort to create chaos.

"My people are protecting our route," Haadiya said.

"There are crowds," Amanda said. "Looks like they're milling around, waiting for instructions. Get back fast."

Instructions that won't come until new leaders get the message.

"We'll leave now," Sofie said. "I don't want to give you an ETA just in case I jinx it."

36

Amanda was sitting at the table working on her pad when Sofie pushed the door to the unit open and led Haadiya inside. The woman looked like a shadow of her normal self. Her hair was drawn back into a bun, and her normally glowing skin was ashy.

Nhu had moved to sit at the end of the table and arranged desk screens to create a separate workstation.

What the fuck?

Sofie glanced at the door to the next unit. Closed. She walked over and used her card to open it. Virgil looked up. He was no worse for wear. "We need to talk," she said, then closed the door. Let him stew over that for a while.

"Okay, what happened?" Sofie asked as she took one of the empty seats.

Haadiya sat next to her, clearly stating his allegiance. Now it was three against one, if Nhu chose to take it that way.

Amanda spoke first. "I checked on him after I woke up. He asked for water, and I gave him some."

"Did he come out?" If he tried to escape, maybe it put Nhu on edge — and with good reason.

"No," she said. "He looked past me, but it's darker in the room. He wouldn't have seen anything beyond a blur. I didn't have the door open long enough for his eyes to adjust."

"Nhu?" Sofie asked to get their attention. They were pretending to focus on work, but the room wasn't big enough for any normal conversation not to be overheard.

They looked up. "When I agreed to that man being held in the next unit, I did not anticipate he would be allowed any freedom. Since I arrived to help, I have been subjected to traitors and the presence of the vermin from the dark streets."

Haadiya stiffened beside Sofie. She wasn't interested in refereeing a fight between two Executives, so she ignored it. "Investigating any serious crime means dealing with people you would normally avoid. The people from the dark streets I've dealt with have been helpful and as eager as anyone to put an end to the violence."

"That doesn't mean I need to be exposed to any of it. You have been quite clear I bring value in this room."

"You aren't being asked to join us outside," Haadiya said. "Your skills lie here."

They glared at him. If Nhu was determined to confront someone, Haadiya was the safest person in the room. He could say what he pleased without fear of retribution. But Sofie wanted to shut this problem down for good. She couldn't keep coming back to the case room to resolve hurt feelings.

"Nhu, something happened that made you change your mind," she said. "When we get through this, the Mallet will be changed one way or another. You don't know who your allies will be in the future, and they could well be people you believe are below your notice."

"I am fully aware that if this situation is poorly resolved, it will not be pleasant for anyone. Don't treat me like a spoiled child, Sofie."

"I didn't mean that," Sofie said. "It's clear Amanda missed something. Tell me what you saw happening."

"Amanda allowed the prisoner an opportunity to escape, or worse, take us hostage." The glare Nhu shot Amanda's way was venomous. "You need to send him away."

"Sofie wants to interrogate him again," Haadiya said. "It is too dangerous and unpredictable on the streets to have him at another site."

"The other units have screens and comms," Nhu said. "No need to go anywhere to ask a few questions."

"There is more to interrogation than questions," Haadiya said. "What is it you need to make this issue go away?"

Sofie let Haadiya talk for now. Nhu seemed to think he was on their side, despite the fact that he was sitting with her and Amanda. If she didn't have to keep the conversation going, she could observe and try to dig out the actual reason Nhu kept trying to be in control or get special treatment.

"I told you, move that man out of our personal space."

There was no real personal space in the units. Although, the room Virgil sat in was supposed to be their sleeping quarters.

"You must understand our reasoning," Haadiya said. "Other than transporting him to another unit, what can we do? Do you need privacy? We can use something in here to close off a corner."

Nhu's eyes widened for a split second.

"He can't get out, Nhu." Sofie waited for the words to sink in.

"Amanda is damaged. He will eventually want more food, or water, or some other trivial thing. She would be easy to overpower. What if he takes control of the comms? What if you come back to him holding a stunner over us?"

"I am perfectly capable of handling him," Amanda said. "I've been taking the pills Sofie brought back and I'm healing fast. I may not be a hundred percent, but even at twenty percent I could kick Virgil's ass."

To her credit, Amanda kept her voice strong. Sofie was not going to send Virgil away regardless of Amanda's ability to stop him from escaping. She needed to talk to him and not just once. The man might know where his peers would go. He was probably still holding on to vital information. If he bought the hype about building a better future, he wouldn't believe that the threat to the Mallet was real.

"The unit has a screen," Sofie said. "We can make sure he's not a threat before we open the door. We won't open the door unless there are two of us here to restrain him. And you can be here, behind the desk screens, if that makes you feel safer."

Nhu stared at the screens and back at Sofie. They looked to Haadiya and then away, probably realizing he was not going to support them. "Very well. I have brought up my concerns. If you think you know better, I will drop the issue."

Sofie didn't believe them, but for now the subject was closed.

37

"Rick's back," Amanda said. "Two people with him."

Announcements that people were arriving gave Sofie a creepy feeling. Like it was a service only available to higher castes, and she would be punished for using it. But knowing who was approaching was vital to their safety. Even with the door locked to anyone without the right pass, they couldn't be sure of their safety. Amanda was not the only hacker on the station, and Nhu wasn't the only one with Executive-level access to systems.

She hurried to the door. Rick pushed it open as she reached for the handle. The two people with him were carrying heavy duffel bags — their weapons. She pushed aside the immediate urge to arrest everyone for having illegal weapons. "Put them there." She pointed to the corner that was quickly becoming their dumping ground for excess supplies.

The two dark streets thugs — she couldn't think of them as anything other than that — dropped the bags and left without raising their eyes from the floor. A pretense that they wouldn't know who was in the room? A nice gesture, but Haadiya would tell them anything he saw fit.

"I know that look," Rick said with a laugh. "Not so easy to put aside your normal thinking about status, right?"

"I thought Haadiya said you'd have transport."

"I changed my mind. It was going to take about an hour to get one big enough. Haadiya already brought his people here, so we're probably not a secret to them anymore."

She didn't see any point in arguing over something that was already done. "Okay. Yeah. Maybe I'll never get used to a new system, but this in-between thing has me distrusting everyone. Looks like you got what we need."

"More than that," Rick said. "Gave Llewelyn the heads up about the weapons."

"I expected you to not share that knowledge," Haadiya said.

"I didn't tell him where or who," Rick said. "I may have hinted that our Executive team members had sources."

Haadiya glanced over at Nhu. "I suppose you had to tell him something."

Rick leaned in to whisper to Sofie. "What's going on?"

She couldn't deny the relationships had changed. Nhu was putting too much effort into ignoring them. "I'll update you later," she said.

"Did Llewelyn have anything to say?" Amanda asked. "It would help to get the official stance on the current situation."

"Oh, yeah, he had plenty to say," Rick answered. "None of it about helping us. He's stuck with a bunch of cops who won't engage the rioters."

If the people who were supposed to quell the violence switched sides, the Mallet was truly lost. She should have realized the message about a better future would be attractive to anyone at any level. "How bad?"

"About ten percent are actively refusing orders. He has no idea who is just pretending to obey."

Punishment would be delayed until after the Mallet was stable again, and maybe forever. "They think they'll get away with it when the new order is established." Sofie didn't have that much faith in the future. "What's he doing with them?"

Rick pulled a package from his pocket. "Taking their weapons and cards. Suspending them. He can't put them in cells because they need the space to hold the rioters."

At least the rioters won't be armed by the converts. If the number of cops drops too low, someone will step in. No, not someone. Ulindia.

"What are those for?" Sofie asked.

Rick pushed the packets of pills around. "Stims. If things get really bad, we can't risk taking time to restore."

"Amanda is just recovering," Sofie said. "We don't know what effect it will have on her." *Or on me.*

"We'll figure it out when we get to the point of taking them," Haadiya said. "And we may not need them at all if we can figure this out fast."

Sofie couldn't quite bring herself to feel that confident. "We need a lead. Right now, all we know is someone is stirring this up, and the only people leading anything are pushing anarchy."

"Not anarchy," Nhu said. They pushed aside a screen to face the team. "It is about taking control and putting what they think of as a better way in place of the current structure. It's always about who is in power. Anarchists just want more power than they have, even if they claim no system is better than what is in place."

Sofie stared at Nhu. They were a pain in the ass, but they did know about power structures. The Executive ran the Mallet for the Elites, who only wanted credits and assumed they would always have the power to generate wealth. The minute they suspected their income streams were threatened, they ran.

"We've been going about this wrong," she said. "We need to talk to the people, not the leaders. We need to spread the truth."

Haadiya chuckled. "You mean we need to spread our truth, Sofie. There is never a single truth. I apologize that I didn't think of it sooner. Perhaps I have been too immersed in the dark streets to remember I am an Executive, with no Elite to remind me."

"Yes," Nhu said. "You have become absorbed in your role of Elite to those criminals."

"Okay, no squabbling," Rick said. "We need to find a way to talk to the rioters."

"We have a way," Haadiya said, nodding toward the connecting door. "Virgil. He should be able to set something up. I'm not sure the rabble know their leadership is gone yet."

"You will not bring him into the case room," Nhu said. They pulled the screen back into place as a barrier.

"We'll go into his space," Sofie said. "Rick, this time you come with me. He might be getting too used to Haadiya's threats."

38

Getting Virgil to agree to contact the people he called his "assistants" was as easy as telling him what was happening outside their location and suggesting what might take place if the sympathetic cops were removed from the equation. He seemed more worried about the possibility that harsher measures were coming to stop the riots than he was about his people accidentally destroying the Mallet. Unless he had a way to ensure it didn't happen, Sofie thought he was taking too big a risk. But he asked for access to a pad and then sent out an invitation to ten people to meet. The link he provided was to a virtual space set up by Amanda.

"How much longer am I going to be locked up here?" Virgil asked as the responses came back. "You need me at this meeting. I want some freedom."

Rick took the pad back and handed it to Sofie. "You aren't getting out of here until the Mallet is peaceful."

"By whose definition?" Virgil asked.

"Let's say 'in control,'" Sofie added. "If we let you attend the meeting, what do you plan to do?" Having him attend was a risk. If he helped persuade his assistants to cooperate, great. But if he tried to take over, there wasn't much anyone could do to stop him. And having him tied up and gagged wasn't the best visual for their purposes.

"It depends on you," Virgil said. "You planning to arrest everyone? Track them down?"

"We don't need you there," Rick said. "We can manage a meeting. No one will know who's in attendance, no one will recognize voices. Your contact taught us a valuable lesson about remaining anonymous."

Sofie left the room without saying more. Rick followed and shut the door on Virgil's sputtering response.

"You and me?" Sofie asked. "For the meeting? Fewer people, clearer message?"

Haadiya reached for the pad. "I want to be there, even if only to observe."

Sofie held it back from him. "Can I trust you to only observe?"

"Probably not," Haadiya said. "But I will try my best to stay quiet."

"Nhu? Do you want to observe?"

"I suppose I should. I can start my research immediately if someone slips and gives us useful information. I will project the meeting on the center screen. You will ensure I am not visible to anyone, even as an outline of a person."

They were carrying this privacy need too far, Sofie thought, but she would not engage in that discussion again. "Sounds like an easy arrangement. Go ahead. In fact, maybe I'm the only person the attendees should be aware of."

"Visible?" Nhu asked.

That could go two ways. Seeing her meant she wasn't trying to hide her identity, but anyone who knew her would think the police were running the show. "Yes," she said.

Time to stop worrying about what the idiots who were trying to destroy her home wanted, and do what she thought right. Being visible was more honest than not. And it was different from what the contact did with the leaders.

THE SCREEN LIT up two minutes before the meeting time. Sofie sat so that both cameras would capture her image. The focus of the recording was set to a tight circle around her. Rick, Amanda, and Haadiya sat close to her, but not on the recording.

The other seats filled rapidly when the time came. All were represented by the same black silhouette.

When everyone was present, Sofie initiated her camera. "Good evening."

Three attendees left the meeting as soon as they saw her.

"Where is Virgil?" The question came from several voices.

"I have a statement to make, and a request." She wasn't going to get distracted by questions. "We have information that this state of violence is being orchestrated by off-Mallet factions. The future promised to you will never be in your favor. We, as the people of the Mallet, need to stop fighting and begin taking control ourselves. The first step is to cease the violent actions."

"You need to bring Virgil into the room," one voice said. It was highly disguised.

"I'm afraid that will not happen, for his safety as well as ours," Sofie said.

"You want us to stop fighting for our lives and our children's future, and you can't prove the person we agreed to follow is alive?"

"He invited you to the meeting," Sofie said. "If he didn't trust us, why would he do that?"

"We don't know what you did to make him obey you," the same voice said. "We are not willing to sit back and let the Elites exploit us any longer."

"The Elites are gone," Sofie said. "This is the time for the rest of us to come together."

"Well fuck you," the voice said. "You're as bad as the Elites. Arresting us on their orders. We know they use you as a weapon. Virgil is gone. I am the new leader. Our contact tells us the new owners will treat us as we deserve."

The silhouettes disappeared all at once. Sofie was left staring at a white screen.

"That didn't help," Haadiya said.

"We tried," Sofie said as she closed the meeting space. "At least we know the contact is still working with someone."

"How stupid are these people?" Haadiya asked. "Don't they realize no one said the Mallet would be a utopia? Being treated as someone else thinks you deserve means being treated poorly, at best."

"They're desperate," Amanda said. "But you did get something confirmed. Someone off-station is planning a takeover. Nhu and I can start searching for likely candidates."

39

Sofie glanced at the newsfeeds on her wrist comm. The streets were still quiet, but one thing bothered her. No cops in sight. She checked the wall of screens as if maybe they would show something different. No cops.

"Can you trace anything from the meeting room?" Rick asked. "Maybe we'll find the identities of the others. Get them in a room like Virgil. Deprogram them?"

"I'll try," Amanda said. "Nhu is more likely to find a corporate link than me, anyway."

"We need to go out and check the streets live," Sofie said.

"You and Rick would be the best for that," Haadiya said. "I will be of more use if Nhu needs a second view on anything they find."

Nhu didn't respond. They were engrossed in something on one of the screens. Whatever it was, they kept it off the wall. Haadiya was more likely to notice if Nhu was doing something other than the task they agreed on, Sofie reasoned. And if the argument about status came up again, he could handle it.

"We won't be long," Sofie said.

Rick looked at the pile of weapons. "Stunners, or do you think we need more?"

"Stunners only, and keep them concealed. Let's avoid confrontation." She tucked her own stunners into their holsters and pulled a jacket over them.

"You want me to use patches, too?" Rick pointed to Sofie's face.

She touched the material on her cheeks. "I forgot I had them on." Normal disruption patches itched after an hour. "These are really good, Haadiya."

"They are expensive, and reusable. Let me take them." He rubbed the patch and Sofie felt the edge curl. Her face was clear within seconds.

"What's worrying you?" Rick asked as the unit door shut behind them.

"Do you think it's a good time for the police presence to be removed from the streets?"

Rick checked his wrist comm, flicking from one feed to another. "Not good. There's no way Llewelyn has this under control."

"You think the feed is being manipulated?" Sofie looked around and then checked her comm for the feed of the street. "It's right for here. No cops, only a few residents passing through."

"Yeah, but look at the area around the station." Rick held his comm close for her to see.

"The bullpen is closed."

"And this one from the next street over."

His comm showed a street much like the one they stood on.

"And these," he said, flicking through the feeds.

"They are all the same," Sofie said. "Someone is looping feed. To cover up some op?"

"Or propaganda. Maybe trying to say 'look how quiet the Mallet is, your battle is lost'?"

"If there is action the feeds don't show, someone will notice, right?"

"No rioter is going to take the time to look at the screens," Rick said. "And if you're in your unit with one going on outside, are you going to check what the media is sending out?"

"Eventually," Sofie said. "So it's a short-term tactic?"

"Or things have settled," he said without any conviction. "Let's look."

The quiet made it too easy to become complacent. Sofie slowed Rick as he hurried to the next square. "Remember what happened to Amanda," she said. "We check before we rush in."

He slowed and glanced down the next side street. "Clear."

She passed and checked the next one, also quiet.

They reached the next square without finding any crowds.

"I don't know why it's so peaceful, but I don't like it," Rick said.

"I keep holding my breath," Sofie said. "And we're whispering."

"Okay, stop for a second." Rick stood, scanning the area. "Is it possible the station is under curfew, and we've missed the notification?"

"You think a curfew would stop the riots? And what about the bullpen? Is it closed because everyone is on the streets keeping order?"

A rumble of voices drew closer.

"I guess not," Sofie said.

Rick pulled her into a doorway as a surge of bodies boiled into the square.

Behind them, a line of gray-overall-clad Ulindia soldiers herded them with stun prods.

Some of the people in the crowd tried to fight, but one touch of the prod had them on the floor jerking from the voltage.

The crowd was herded forward in the direction of the jail. Then the square was empty but for a handful of people still recovering from the stun prods.

Sofie ran to the closest victim. She was still breathing, and her spasms were weaker. "Rick, make sure everyone else is okay."

She waited until the woman could speak before asking, "What was that all about?"

"Fucking assholes showed up a while ago. They find more than a few people together, they force them to a holding cell. Don't care if you are just trying to get to work. Don't listen to anyone."

This was not going to fix things. Using that much force without provocation was just going to push people to join the rebellion.

"Can you get home?" she asked.

"Gotta get to work, gotta keep the Mallet running." The woman struggled to her feet and ran off.

"They'll be fine," Rick said, returning to Sofie. "I guess we know why the cops are gone."

"You think Llewelyn told them about us? Where we're working?" Sofie asked.

"Not a chance." Rick tipped his head toward the case room. "We should get out of here before someone decides we might be a problem."

40

"I can make you safe in the dark streets," Haadiya said when Sofie explained what they saw.

She looked around the room and considered. The equipment would stay because it was too much to move. If they ran into a group of rioters, they wouldn't be able to get away fast if they were carrying screens and all the cables. And, maybe worse, the Ulindia guys would pull them in on the suspicion that they were looters. But the investigation didn't need the screens beyond giving Nhu and Amanda a way to do their research efficiently.

They couldn't abandon Virgil here, but it was also unwise to move him. Sofie held out hope he would still be of use.

"It would help to keep us working," Rick said. "If Ulindia forces Llewelyn to tell them about us, we wouldn't be here for anyone to stop us."

"Why would they stop us?" Nhu asked, finally joining the conversation. "We are trying to stabilize the Mallet."

For someone who played political games all day, Nhu could be naive, Sofie thought. "They could be working for whoever is pushing the violence to the edge. Or, maybe they don't want anyone interfering with their plan to save us. Have you found anything?"

"I'm reviewing the financial statements of our current customers, nothing yet," Nhu said. "I have requested a list of newly formed companies in our industry, or any that have connections with one of our clients."

"And?" *Why can't they be more forthcoming?*

"Nothing so far." Nhu glanced toward Virgil's door. "I will not enter the dark streets. And I will not be alone here with him."

Not again. "We haven't decided anything," Sofie said.

"My people can gather intelligence and report back here," Haadiya said. "We don't need to be on site for it."

"Your people have not yet provided any information we can use," Nhu said. "Why do you think that will change?"

"Because at some point they must find something," Haadiya snapped back. "You have not found any useful tips either, but I have faith that you will, and so we are patient."

Why didn't Nhu stop stirring the pot?

Haadiya's comments helped Sofie come to her decision. This was the last opportunity they had to move. The case was taking too long to solve. From here on out, every action needed to be focused on stopping the violence, not on dealing with the latest rumor or a problem someone else could solve easily. Or a hissy fit from someone who should be mature enough to compromise.

Sofie slapped her hand on the table to get everyone's attention. "Stop bickering. This is too important for egos."

Four heads turned in her direction, but no one spoke. Their expressions showed shock, not anger. Time to take control.

"There's no good choice," she said. "We keep losing sight

of the fact that we are supposed to be a team, and it's getting in the way of clear thinking."

It wasn't just Nhu; Haadiya was trying to take control as well. Going to the dark streets gave him that power. But he had been helpful, and Nhu hadn't so far.

Rick shrugged. "You have a point. But we can't afford to lose communication."

"This Ulindia is not like us," Amanda said. "You know, they're more like a military force. They see everyone who isn't on their team as the enemy. We see residents of the Mallet, no matter their crimes."

And the military was less likely to worry about the future of the station. "We don't know their orders," Sofie said.

"You can't take the chance," Haadiya said. "I can protect you all against whatever they throw at us. I can provide you with people to keep you safe, which means you can focus on solving the problem, not worrying about when the next riot will trap you."

Sofie knew she should let everyone say their piece, but right now the team needed a leader. And leaders made decisions with the information at hand and didn't try to second guess every possibility.

"This is what we do," she said. "Amanda and I will go with Haadiya. Amanda has recovered enough to do more than research. Nhu, you and Rick work from here. If Ulindia's people find you, then an Executive and their personal bodyguard is all they'll see."

"They will find the prisoner," Nhu said. "What reason would we have to keep someone locked up?"

"We say he's your assistant and is being punished for insubordination," Rick said. "Virgil won't argue because he's safer here."

"We'll keep in touch through our comms," Sofie said. "Rick is here to help you, Nhu."

"Amanda could do that," Nhu said.

"But we need her skills in the dark streets," Sofie said. "One technical genius in each location means we can't be cut off."

The argument was weak, but Sofie figured Rick's charm might keep Nhu from tossing Virgil to the street.

"And you have your privacy and time to focus," Rick said. "I promise not to distract you. I can pick my way through the screens while you look through legal documents. I can let Amanda know if I find anything she needs to fix."

Having him here also meant he could interrogate Virgil when Sofie needed answers.

"Let's get our stuff," she said, not waiting for any other discussion to start.

41

"Let my people ask the questions," Haadiya said for the third time. "They fit in."

Sofie stood at the screen in Haadiya's dark streets quarters. This one showed a different scene than her wrist comm. It was pulling feed from the drones still operating in parts of the Mallet. Very few of them had survived the purge. The Ulindia people were controlling the message, and they wanted people to think the violence was over. Her comm showed people going about usual business. The screen showed clusters of people, some being held for arrest by security people with powerful weapons, some slipping from street to street toward a common destination. Haadiya's screens were more likely to show reality, Sofie thought.

"Who owns the drones?" she asked, turning away to check the room.

His quarters were big, three or four units joined together. This room was for meeting people. The next was a kitchen, the one beyond a bathroom facility that somehow overrode the water restrictions, and beyond that was a space dedicated to a bed and wardrobe. He'd managed to replicate his Executive luxuries in the dark streets.

"I do," he said. "They are camouflaged. Sensors keep them in the shadows unless there is no movement in their range."

"They can still be hacked," Amanda said. "How are you sure if any of the feeds are real or not?"

"I get frequent live reports." He pulled out a chair and sat at a table.

Amanda sat at a desk that attached to the wall, checking something on her pad. Three other pads sat beside her. "I've connected all the devices," she said. "You'll be able to watch us. We need disguises and small stunners."

Sofie turned back to the screen, hiding her smile. Perhaps Haadiya would get the hint and stop trying to keep them inside.

"We'll take an escort," she said. "One person. The rest of your people can continue their efforts. We're going to listen, not interrogate. If people get a chance to explain their goals, maybe they'll slip up and give us a name."

"You know why the fools are rioting; you're taking a risk going out there for a hope of a clue," he said, tapping his comm. He read something and said, "Your new clothes should be here in a few minutes. Do you want patches?"

"Are any people wearing them?" Amanda asked.

Sofie searched the feeds for faces. "Unless someone is projecting a different face, no. So, we'll stand out if we wear them."

"That's an interesting idea," Haadiya said. "Patches that match the skin so they can fool not only the cameras, but also the naked eye. There's always money to be made."

"We have to survive first," Sofie said.

"A good businessperson doesn't stop looking for ways to

make money." He joined Sofie at the screen. "So, why do you want people to tell you why they're putting everyone at risk? You've heard the message."

He must know the answer, Sofie thought. His tone was more like that of a professor testing a student than someone looking for real information.

"Messages get garbled. I don't believe everyone out there is fighting for a new and better future. Life on the Mallet doesn't make you altruistic or hopeful. If we start hearing consistent messages, we may find a trail to the organizer. That contact Virgil told us about."

"I should come," Haadiya said.

"We need you here," Sofie said. "If something happens to you, Nhu will be the only person left to lead the Mallet."

"That would be tragic," Haadiya said. A chime sounded. "Perhaps it would be better if you weren't known by everyone here. Go to the kitchen while I accept the package."

So, he doesn't completely trust his people.

Sofie listened to the voices in the next room as she and Amanda waited. The conversation was muffled and far too long for Haadiya to be simply accepting a package.

"Are you sure you're up to this?" she asked Amanda. "It might get difficult out there."

"I took some of the stims, and I'm healed. Your doctor's meds were stronger than any I've used before," Amanda said. "I wouldn't say I was ready if I wasn't, you know that."

"Okay. Let's hope we get some answers."

"Yes, and avoid being arrested."

The door opened, and Haadiya passed them two packages. "Your disguises. I've told your escort to be here in ten minutes."

42

Sofie and Amanda left the dark streets through the hidden exit she'd used before. The street outside was crowded, but no sign of gray coveralls or armed police meant less chance of violence, as far as she was concerned. Their escort had slipped out first to confirm the street was safe.

Now, Sofie leaned against a closed stim-juice stall and watched the people milling around in the square. Amanda stood beside her, occasionally commenting quietly.

"You want to try that cluster across the square?" Amanda asked. "People are wandering in and out, maybe they won't get too suspicious."

Choosing where to start was important. If they wandered in and out of the groups too quickly, someone would notice and get suspicious. In fact, other people were doing the same thing as they were. "Check out the man standing in the snack bar door. He's not interested in any group. We need to make sure the spotter, or whatever he is, doesn't expose us."

"He's not watching the square that closely," Amanda

said. "He's probably there as a lookout for the authorities. There's someone at each corner."

It made sense to have early warning of the gray coveralls. "You think maybe this is recruiting?"

"It doesn't seem that organized."

"Okay, I think you're right. Our best option is to head to the cluster you pointed out," Sofie said. "I'll go in first. You can wander by or go off to a different one. It's better if we look like individuals rather than a team, right?"

"You go now," Amanda whispered.

"It isn't right," a woman muttered as Sofie joined the group. "We got to get our people in charge, now."

"How are we going to do that?" a man asked. "You got some big guns somewhere?"

"Only way to get what we deserve is fight," another woman said. "The riots got everyone's attention. Now we fight harder."

Sofie slipped deeper into the group, keeping her eyes down to avoid being drawn into a conversation. She noticed Amanda peel away to join a smaller group.

"You forget we're on a space station?" the first man said. "We fight too hard, they can space us. Or we break the wrong thing, and we space everyone."

At least someone's talking sense.

"We got to get surgical," he continued. "Pick a target and shut it down. Keep the riots small and away from places we need to keep safe."

"Protect the people working to keep things running," a different man said. "If we win and the station is shut down, we lose. We lose, and they need us to run the Mallet, so we survive."

Until the new bosses bring in more amenable, or more desperate, people to replace us. Sofie didn't have any faith that she would survive an upheaval. Maybe the doctors, judges, Executive — those who stayed — would remain, but no guarantees for anyone else.

"If we aren't ready to take over," the first woman said, "nothing changes. We need to pick our own Elite."

"No more Elite," the second man said. "No more castes. Everyone works, everyone has a voice, no one gets to profit from our pain and sweat."

"And no more debt," a new woman said. "We all start fresh."

The crowd was getting bigger, and that would attract attention. Sofie maneuvered her way to the edge of the group and wandered around the square looking for Amanda, and another crowd to infiltrate.

Amanda was talking to their escort. A group of men and women in their twenties gathered near the closest entrance. People who were not yet ground down by years of hard, unrewarding work. She wouldn't pass for one of them but needed to know if they had the same opinions and arguments as the others. She shuffled past the group, feeling them watch her as she headed to a doorway only a few feet farther along. She kept her eyes on the ground and tried to project an image of exhaustion.

"No more waiting, right?" a young man said. "They don't listen to us. Keep rounding us up and locking us away. We hit them back. Hard."

"I'm not going to die for the cause," another man said. "I want to be alive when we win. I plan to run this station, not go back to the line."

She listened as the others in the group muttered similar sentiments. The message wasn't as distorted as she hoped. Underneath the different plans was the belief that the Mallet was up for grabs. That a new leadership would come from the upheaval. That life would be better for everyone. Did they remember how life had been only a week ago? Probably not. If they did, they'd remember that the Mallet would never change, the people in charge would exploit the workers, and greed would make people do stupid things.

She glanced up to see Amanda standing beside their escort, glaring at her. The message was clear: time to get out. She heard the sound of boots a second before the lookouts shouted a warning. The danger was coming from behind her.

Sofie pushed off the wall and ran across the square, getting halfway to her destination before anyone else reacted. She could see the top of Amanda's head over the people who were now competing for the fastest route out. She used her elbows and shoulders to fend off the bodies that threatened to overwhelm her.

A hand reached through a gap. Sofie grabbed it and let their escort pull her the rest of the way to relative safety.

"We go back now," the woman said, giving Sofie a shove in the direction of the dark streets.

———————

43

S ofie's wrist comm chimed as she stepped through the secret entrance to the dark streets and safety. "Wait," she said to Amanda and their guard. "It's Rick. We might be going back out."

The gatekeeper shook his head at her. "No one but me stays in here."

She ignored him and answered the call. "Is this urgent?"

"You busy?" Rick asked.

"Just not welcome at my current location. Can you give me time to get clear?"

"Call me back?"

"No. I only need a few seconds." She nudged Amanda and followed their guard to the street outside. "Is it safe to take the call here?"

"No one is around." The guard stepped away. "Take your call, I'll give you privacy."

Amanda moved closer to Sofie. "Turn the volume down. We can lean in close so no one can hear."

She felt foolish for being so cautious, but if any news Rick might have for them got into the wrong hands, it could mean failure. Haadiya might pretend to have complete trust in his dark street residents, but she didn't. Even if his trust was founded, she'd spent too many years thinking of this area as a cesspit of depravity to change now.

"Okay, go ahead," she whispered to Rick.

"I need Haadiya back in the case room." Rick also whispered. He was hiding his call.

"Where are you?" Sofie asked. "What happened?"

"I'm still here. In the middle room. Virgil is still locked up. Nhu is the problem."

"What did they do?"

"Nothing outright, but they've been bent over their screens since you left. I know they're sending communications, but when I try to trace the calls, nothing shows up."

Sofie looked at Amanda, trying to assess her health. She had the skills to uncover Nhu's activities, and despite her assurances about being healed, she looked ready to crawl into bed and sleep for a week.

"Don't look at me like that," Amanda said.

"You could hack her comms," Sofie said.

"I need to be here with you. If I stop moving, I'm going to fall asleep. You think sending me to stare at a screen is the best idea?"

"I wanted Haadiya," Rick said. "I need someone Nhu might listen to. They're acting like I'm not even in the unit."

"We need him here," Sofie said. "His people follow his orders. I don't think they'll do that for me. They know I'm a cop. And every single one of them gives me that glare of defiance before they do as he asks."

"I can only watch Nhu. We need to know who they are calling." Rick put the call on hold.

"What the fuck?" Amanda asked.

"I guess Nhu isn't entirely ignoring him. What do you think we should do?"

"Maybe Haadiya has someone who can hack the comms? You got it right about needing him here. No one will do what either of us needs without him issuing the commands. I don't blame them. We're the enemy, right?"

Rick rejoined the call. "Nhu came in to ask me to make them some food. Like I'm a servant now," Rick said. "This is getting worse. I need someone on their level to... I don't know, control doesn't seem possible, maybe persuade them to act like they're on our side?"

"I'll ask Haadiya about a hacker. If he sends someone to help, can you deal with Nhu's objections?"

"Oh yeah, they'll love that. I can find some reason we need help from the dark streets. How's it going out there?"

Sofie hoped Rick was right. She didn't need to be worried about Nhu undermining the team while she searched for a solution. "The message seems to be consistent that the new leaders will be loving and nurturing. Some variation in the wonderful promises, but not enough to fragment the movement. We need to find the real power behind this contact."

"Okay. Let me know if Haadiya agrees to help. I won't say anything until I know someone is coming."

"If you think Nhu is really working against us, lock them up." Sofie didn't think Nhu would act to sabotage the Mallet, but they had their own priorities like all the Executives did. And if she was honest with herself, not just the Executives — everyone on the Mallet was out to make their own lives better.

"I'll keep an eye on Nhu, but I can't guarantee I'll notice if they are doing something dangerous."

"I'll reach out to you to let you know what Haadiya says." Sofie ended the call.

"You know, a hacker doesn't need to be on-site to work," Amanda said. "Unless Nhu has cut access from outside, the system is open to manipulation."

"And if they have?" Sofie asked.

"That can be cracked too. Let's get back to Haadiya."

44

Solving a case by hacking information was not Sofie's style. She liked tracking down the perpetrator by following clues and talking to people. But she had to accept that this case wasn't going to work out that way. She still thought of it as a case, even though it was more like an intelligence operation. It helped her to feel some hope they'd solve it, because she had no experience with spying, and no experience equaled no confidence.

But her preference wasn't helping to solve anything. This wasn't the kind of crime she dealt with on a normal basis, so no informant or even experience guiding her. It definitely felt like everyone was a perpetrator, but maybe that was just in Maintenance.

Sofie let her thoughts float as she followed Amanda and their guard back to Haadiya's residence. Sometimes drawing back from the chase let her see details she missed with too tight a focus. This time it gave her nothing. Normally she wouldn't feel sympathy for criminals, but life on the Mallet was shitty. Change was needed, and she wanted the station to survive the transition.

"I'll be out here," their guard said as she pushed on Haadiya's door contact plate. "I like not knowing your plans. Means I don't have a wrong side to choose. I just do what I'm told unless I don't like the orders."

What kind of life had the woman lived to make her so passive? Sofie didn't comment; the woman was allowed to make her own choices.

She explained Rick's call to Haadiya. "I don't have an answer for him."

Haadiya sent a message on his pad before saying, "My hacker will be here in a few minutes. He will find out what Nhu is doing."

"And then?" Amanda asked. "Can you control them? Even if it's innocent, they're getting in the way."

Amanda looked ready to pass out.

"Maybe you should grab a nap," Sofie said. "Or at least sit down while we talk."

"I could use another stim," she said, but did sit on the sofa. "If I fall asleep, don't forget to wake me."

Sofie nodded and then turned back to Haadiya. "Can you? Manage Nhu?"

"I don't think they see me as an equal," he said. "I am no longer an Executive liaison. I am the boss of the dark streets."

"Nhu isn't an Executive either," Sofie said. "No Elite, no liaison."

"Yes, and as I said, I have a role, they do not. It makes a difference even if they look down on me."

"Amanda is right. Even if they are playing games to gain an advantage in the new structure, they're getting in the way. If we aren't successful, there's no new structure. There's no caste system in death." *At least I hope not.*

"Sofie, just because I'm helping you save the station

doesn't mean I'm not ambitious. I won't be happy if Nhu rises and I don't. I will help you with Nhu, but my suggestion is to lock them away until this is over. I am more use to you here than I am babysitting Nhu."

Nhu shouldn't need a babysitter.

"Let's see what your hacker finds. It's not like we've got any leads to follow. I feel like we're going to be running after shadows as the station blows apart."

He smiled and patted her shoulder. "You should eat. Your spirits need a lift. I think you and Nhu have more in common than you think. While they are ignoring the current situation for the future, you are ignoring the future to focus on the current situation."

Is that true? Should I be able to figure out what Nhu is up to because we are so similar?

"Without us solving the current situation, we have no future," she said. "But yes, I'm starving." She looked over at Amanda, who was now curled on her side, asleep.

He led her to the kitchen, where he took a meal package from the cupboard and pulled the tab to heat the contents. "You have a moment right now to think. What is your place in the new Mallet?"

Sofie tasted the stew. Much more flavor than what she could access normally. The inequality of the Mallet was ingrained in every single aspect of life.

Haadiya's question bothered her because she'd never thought beyond her current role. "No matter what changes, there's always a need for cops. I like what I do."

"If you could make one change, what would it be?" He poured her a stim-juice.

"That's the problem: choosing one," she said. "I agree that there's too much power in too few hands. We need more balance. Sure, the work won't change, but why do the workers have to be so exploited?"

"You should be one of the leaders," Haadiya said, "in the future. Oh, here is my hacker."

Sofie tossed the meal container into the recycler and joined Haadiya in the living room. Amanda still slept on the couch. A man sat across the desk from Haadiya, clearly waiting for her to give him something.

"I need your codes to get in fast," he said. "You want it fast, right? No waiting for me to get in a back door?"

Sofie looked at Haadiya. She couldn't hand over codes that gave this hacker access to everything.

"Just kidding, lady," the hacker said. "You can set me up, right? Like a user. You give me access to what I need, and I do my thing."

"I guess I lost my sense of humor," Sofie said. "I need my pad and a name."

"Call me Newboy," he said. "I need admin rights for the comms in your secret bunker."

Sofie logged in and looked for the case room. There was only one access level available: user. "No admin," she said.

"Lemme see," Newboy said. He grabbed her pad and sighed. "You need to set the access in a different place." He typed on her pad before Sofie could stop him. "Here we go. And I'm in."

She made a mental note to have Amanda check his work when she woke. "How long will it take?"

"The target is Nhu Eckerman, right?"

"Yes. And only them." Sofie ignored Haadiya, who was watching them work from across the room. If she focused on what Newboy was doing, maybe she could prevent him doing something outside what she needed.

"Okay, so this Nhu is making a lot of calls. Give me a

second." Newboy kept up a running narration as he coded searches. Five minutes of unintelligible comments and he straightened from his slump over his screen and pointed. "Yeah, here's the locations. That help?"

The list showed that Nhu was almost constantly reaching out. If it was to gather intelligence on the source of the upheaval, it would be great. But one location stood out. Sofie pointed to it. "Any chance of a recording, or transcript?"

"Erased. But the call was only a few minutes."

That's all it took to tell people their future was going to be what they deserve.

45

The trip back to the case room was a blur. Sofie struggled to keep her focus on the journey as she thought back through all the times Nhu pretended to be on their side. How they had manipulated the team to be alone when Sofie was at the meeting with the contact. How they found information in bits and pieces when it was clear they knew exactly what was going on.

Haadiya and Amanda kept pace with her as the guards cleared the way. Sofie didn't care what actions they took. The faster she could get to Nhu and confront them, the faster the Mallet would be safe.

"Are you going to interrogate Nhu in private?" Haadiya asked.

"They know the tactics, so I'm not wasting my time finding a private place. If there is a good reason for this betrayal, they won't mind telling all of us."

"You want a guard to join us?" Amanda asked. "It might help intimidate them. If Nhu thinks they can work around us, maybe some hard-assed, heavily armed criminals will push them over the edge."

Or be a diversion. "I think the guards should stay outside," she said, coming to a stop. "We're here. Let me take the lead. Haadiya, I need your Executive perspective but don't explain unless I ask. Amanda, take over the comms and let Rick know what's going on."

"And Virgil?" Amanda asked. "Nhu wanted him gone because he might recognize them, right? Do you want to bring him out of the room?"

"Not until I say so." Sofie didn't want him causing problems if he did recognize Nhu. She wanted them feeling alone and facing a united enemy. She pressed her card on the contact plate and stepped inside the room.

"Nhu, move away from the comms." Sofie kept her voice level.

"You found out what's going on?" Rick asked.

Sofie nodded but left the details for Amanda to explain. Nhu narrowed their eyes at Sofie, then glanced at Haadiya. He didn't react, and that seemed to get through to Nhu.

"Where am I supposed to go?" they asked. "What are you accusing me of?"

"Haadiya, put a chair against the wall for Nhu. Amanda, do your thing with the comms."

Nhu didn't put up any resistance, but Sofie didn't see any sign that they were about to confess. She heard Amanda talking quietly to Rick, then tuned out everything but Nhu and Haadiya. She stepped toward Nhu, close enough to violate their private space and make them uncomfortable. Nhu leaned away a little but showed no other discomfort.

"We hacked your comms," Sofie said. No need to warm up to the subject. "You are behind the riots. You are taking orders from someone. Just tell me who and we can end this situation."

"What makes you think your hacker is truthful? It would be easy to plant an evidence trail to me."

Sofie looked to Haadiya to answer the question.

"I trust the man," he said. "If I find he lied to us, he will die. He knows that."

"I trust Haadiya," Sofie said.

"Because you know him?" Nhu laughed. "You know me too. Why am I the one sitting here? He runs the biggest criminal enterprise on the Mallet."

"True, but he has been nothing but helpful. Telling us his identity was a big risk. For all he knows, we'll be arresting him as soon at the Mallet settles down. He hasn't kept his ambitions secret."

"At least you're savvy enough to know he still has ambitions," Nhu said. "What do you want to know?"

"You admit it?" It was too easy. Sofie expected Nhu to deny their role in the violence until there was no option but to tell the truth.

"There is no benefit to me in pretending. Yes, I am the contact for the riot leaders. I am controlling the transition."

"Who do you answer to?"

"The same people as always. The Elites." Nhu relaxed in the seat. "They want to keep the income stream but are tired of living on the Mallet. Who isn't?"

"So, there is no residency clause?" Sofie wished she could ask Haadiya to explain but Nhu needed to remain the focus of the questioning.

"There is. Not everything I told you was a lie." They licked their lips. "I would like some water."

"I want answers that will help save the Mallet and everyone on it, including you." Sofie nodded to Haadiya to bring Nhu a drink. "Are you going to tell us?"

"I understand why it is difficult for you to figure out,

Sofie. You are not expected to think about long-term strategy. I am surprised that Haadiya has not told you."

Why does every criminal in an interrogation play games? Even when they want to tell you how smart they are, there are all these little distractions and snipes. "I want to hear it from you."

Nhu accepted the plastic bottle of water and took a long drink. They put the bottle on the floor and sat straighter. "The Elites have formed a new corporation. This entity will buy the rights to the Mallet from the individual families with an amendment to the clause. Only one representative of each family will be required to live on the Mallet. That representative can be appointed from outside the family and caste. That person will receive compensation commensurate with the profit flow."

"And you want to be one of these representatives," Sofie said. "And the violence is to discourage other corporations from making a bid until the plan is complete."

Nhu smiled. "See? You are smart enough to figure it out."

"If the Mallet is destroyed, how will anyone profit?"

"There has been no permanent damage to the station, few injuries. We will need the workers on the line when we are done." Nhu reached for the bottle again. "The Ulindia team is prepared to take action if I misjudge the situation. We have kept the violence to Maintenance so it will be easy to subdue the crowd."

"And the competition is sitting back and waiting?" Haadiya asked. "You haven't told us everything, Nhu. Torque was told the evacuation was temporary, so at least one of our clients knows, or is really behind it."

They sighed. "You are right. We must finish this soon. The competition is gathering resources. This takeover may be secret here, but outside the Mallet... news is spreading.

And the grace period information was true. We only have three days to get the contract signed."

And that meant Nhu and their Elite masters would lose control of the crowds before they could cool tempers. And someone new would own the Mallet, someone who might just be worse.

46

"Am I to be locked away?" Nhu asked with all the self-righteousness of someone who believed they were being wrongly accused.

"I need to think," Sofie said. "Just sit here until I know what I'm going to do."

"I'll watch Nhu," Haadiya said. "May I give you one piece of advice?"

"Sure," Sofie said. *It's not like I have to do more than listen to it.*

"This changes what we need to do," he said. "We aren't trying to return to the status quo. We are building the future. I know you think Nhu and I are only trying to ensure we have power, but remember that we know how the Mallet works."

"I will ask you for help," she said, "but you are not the only ones who know how the Mallet works. And your view is from the Executive level."

She didn't wait for him to answer. She didn't have time to really process what had happened, but she wasn't going to define the future of the Mallet by herself. Most of their problems came up because someone thought they could do just that. Building the future from a cop's perspective was probably worse than doing it from an Elite's or Executive's. And she'd never signed up to be a savior.

She opened the door to Virgil's cell and stepped inside, closing everyone out.

"What happened?" he asked.

"Why do you think something happened?"

"You wouldn't be here if nothing has changed. Is the Mallet safe?"

Sofie told him everything.

"I fucking knew the Elites were behind it," Virgil said. "I just didn't want to believe it."

"The promises were powerful," Sofie said. "If I bring you into the other room and let you help, will I be making a mistake?"

Her words surprised him, and she watched the internal battle play out on his face. The frown deepened, and then gradually cleared. She knew he would set a price; this was the Mallet, after all.

"Can I trust you to let the last few days go? That the new world won't start with shoving anyone in a cell? Or worse?"

An acceptable price. "If I could punish someone for this, it would be the Elites. You and your friends are safe if we win. I can't promise anything if we lose."

Virgil pushed his hands forward. "Then we have a deal. Cut me loose."

Sofie released the restraints and unlocked the door. Virgil followed her out and waited for her to control the team. Now she needed everyone else to agree as easily as Virgil did.

"Everyone has a voice," she said. "We will find a way to

shut this violence down before it goes too far, or before the Ulindia team makes it worse."

"Why should we trust this criminal?" Nhu asked.

It's like they forgot we know they're the one pushing the mob. "Because I trust him to help."

Nhu crossed their arms but didn't say anything. Sofie thought they were stuck in this role and only acting like a spoiled child because they were unsure how to move away from it. Sofie had no intention of wasting time to coax Nhu into the group.

"We need to find other people to help," she said, "but we can't just ask anyone unless we have a goal."

"The plan must be to save the Mallet," Virgil said. "Nothing else will attract followers."

"We aren't looking for followers," Amanda said. "Unless I'm way off the mark, we need to work together. No more vague promises about the future."

Sofie held back her words. If she spoke now, it put her more firmly in a leadership role, meaning that people would agree or disagree with her. If they were a team, everyone's ideas were valid.

"Virgil, you know who should work with us," Rick said. "How do we get to them?"

"I can send messengers," Haadiya said.

"What message will they carry?" Nhu asked, their petulance gone as they engaged in the discussion. "We cannot sit here all day talking. Actions are needed."

"Actions without directions?" Amanda asked. "We need to tell everyone who is behind this mess. We need ideas on how to connect with the corporations. To negotiate the deal."

That was exactly right, Sofie thought. "Yes. Right now, every person on the Mallet has more power than anyone trying to take over," she said. "We'll never be in a better position to negotiate than we are today."

"Who with?" Haadiya asked. "It's a good strategy. But who will we contact?"

"How will we?" Virgil asked.

"We'll figure that out," Sofie said. "But the who? Easy. We know the Elites. They know the Mallet. Any new owner — fuck, I hate to think we're owned — won't grasp the reality. The Elites want the income stream without being here. If they win, we know that means life will be worse than before because they aren't in the same danger as us."

Haadiya looked at Nhu and then Sofie before saying, "We also have a way to contact the Elites."

Nhu gave a small smile. Sofie saw triumph in the expression.

"Not yet," Sofie said. "And no warning to them, Nhu. First, we bring more people together and figure out what we want. Then we start negotiating."

"Someone from every level," Virgil said. "Every caste with an equal voice."

"Yes. That's the message." Sofie felt for the first time that they would succeed.

47

Having a reasonable next step didn't make it any easier. Without the normal communications lines, Sofie didn't know who to reach out to first.

"We can't just put out a call," she said. "Right now, we're hidden and safe from interference. We need to let Llewelyn know when we make some progress so he can start taking control again."

"The Elites don't count," Virgil said. "They aren't here, and this mess is all because of them. So how many people do we need?"

Answering that question might just help decide who they needed, too. Virgil was not just a puppet; he really thought they could win. "If we count Manufacturing and Maintenance as separate castes," she said, "five representatives?"

"No. It's not that clear," Haadiya said. "Look, the Executive is pretty homogeneous. We might be chasing different ways to meet our goals, but we all want power and a smooth-running Mallet. But that's not true of the rest of the station." He looked at Nhu. "Am I wrong?"

They raised an eyebrow and turned to Sofie as if asking for permission to talk. Apparently, the pout wasn't finished. Sofie nodded, determined not to be drawn off topic.

"This is basically true," they said. "Are you suggesting that our whole caste be represented by you?"

"Both of you," Sofie said, cutting off Haadiya's response. "This is only about forming a council to start negotiations. We don't need to bring in dozens of people, but Haadiya is right. We can't just look at this through the caste system. I mean, Support holds doctors, educators, and scientists. They will all want a voice, and should get one. Authority is lawyers, judges, and police. I don't know if any of us is the right person to represent all of those roles."

How would they know when there were enough people?

"Look," Virgil said, "it's not that complicated. We already have a contact with the Elites off-station. We don't have to pick the representative for every role for this step. I know a few names in Maintenance and a contact in Manufacturing who can add more."

"What about Petra?" Amanda asked. "She would be good at negotiation, or know someone who would be."

"I've got a person in legal," Rick said. "But we're forgetting something. Where are we going to do this? It's not safe for people to move around right now."

It was never just one problem, Sofie thought. "Nhu, who is your contact off-station?"

"Lilianna Ruiz, of course. I don't deal with other families." Uncrossing their arms, Nhu leaned forward. "I can contact her and set a meeting. Virtual would work."

"No," Rick said. "We need to be ready before you call her. We set the time and the agenda."

Nhu smiled. "You forget she is a Pratham. Do you think she will simply bend to your demands?"

"Yes," Sofie said. "She'll have no choice. Is the Ruiz family representing all the Elites?"

"It is part of the corporation setup. The families each run the company for a year. Their decision-making powers are limited, but she will shepherd this through."

One problem solved.

"Do I need to lock you up to keep you from calling her?" Sofie asked.

"Please do not do that," Nhu said quietly. "Amanda can lock me out of the system until you are prepared to begin. I still advise not simply dumping this on Lilianna."

"You'll give input when we have our team," Sofie said. "We need to reach out. Is there a section we're missing?"

"I will represent the Executive and the dark streets," Haadiya said. "I've been doing it all my life, so it's no strain on me."

"What do we tell them?" Amanda asked. "To convince someone to join us, how much information is safe to reveal?"

"I don't know about the other castes," Virgil said, "but I will tell my contacts that we have a solution, and that I need them to help save the Mallet. And that it will not be the same as before."

Everyone thought that the higher castes were more mature and capable of seeing facts rather than emotions. Nhu and Haadiya were examples of how false that assumption was. "A good message," Sofie said, "for all of us. We need to do this fast."

"I'll need a pad," Virgil said.

Sofie handed him a spare one and then moved away from the group. She needed a bit of peace to talk to her contacts, and everyone was talking on the comms.

48

Even with all the chaos in Maintenance, it took less than an hour to form the council. People were tired of the uncertainty and the real fear that each breath would be their last. The council — Sofie had no other word for it — convened in a private meeting space. No one hid behind a distortion field, but no names were displayed. She hoped that meant they were committed to the idea of saving the Mallet, and understood this was only the first step.

Nhu was out of camera view, but they could hear the conversation. Rick sat with his own pad next to them, ready to intervene if they decided the risk of being locked up was worth interrupting. Each of the people in the room joined from their own pads.

Facilitating the meeting fell to Sofie.

"Thank you for trusting us enough to attend," she said after introducing herself and the others in the room.

"We all want the riots to end," a man said. He was one of Virgil's contacts. "If you have a way to do that, I'm listening."

A woman wearing the coveralls of a Manufacturing supervisor agreed.

"We have an idea," Sofie said. "It needs input, and we must move fast."

"Tell us what you know," Petra Starlight said. "I'm sure you will keep details back until we commit, Sofie, but if we must move fast, we need to know where we are starting from."

"This violence is being sustained with lies," Sofie said. "It's a takeover attempt. We are in a position to control at least some of the aspects of the transition and change the way the Mallet works."

"Who's stupid enough to risk destroying something they want?" a Maintenance worker asked. "We should drag them out to the streets and make them see the violence firsthand."

"This is coming from off-station. And I think the idea of the violence is to discourage competition."

"So, this mystery buyer has some way of shutting down the riots." This came from a woman in the dark suit of a judge. "The fools who believed their lies are going to face retribution, not reward, when the new owners arrive."

"We aren't fools," the Manufacturing supervisor shouted. "We're just desperate. You live our lives for a day, you'll understand."

"Your role is determined by your aptitude," a different woman said. A teacher, Sofie thought, although she was in street clothes and not the light blue coveralls of her position.

"This is what they want," Sofie said, keeping her voice neutral to defuse the anger long enough to be heard. "We must decide to leave the past behind. We are on the Mallet. We are all on the same side."

"We have no power," the Manufacturing representative said. "What's my guarantee the lower castes will get some?"

Everyone stopped talking to hear her answer. The question was good, but Sofie hadn't thought of how to answer it. There was no guarantee. She was not going to mimic the Elites' vague promises of a better future. She only had the truth and a hope that these people would understand there were no guarantees.

"I know the leaders of the riots have been promised a better life," she said. "We all want that. But a better life isn't going to be imposed on us. If we allow this takeover to go ahead without our voices, we give up any power before we even ask for it."

The audience was still listening.

"I don't know what a better life means to people in the lower castes, or the higher, or even my own. Each of us has an individual dream. We need people to form a council to negotiate, to define the minimums. Because no matter what, ore will need to be refined, the station will need to be maintained. We will need doctors."

"But not every job will survive if we don't take steps now," Haadiya said. "Think about it. What happens if we are all put on the same level? We all become Maintenance and Manufacturing? Medical aide can come from outside; policing and justice systems are the same. Our debts will not be forgiven or decreased; more likely, we will all carry a bigger burden than before."

The Maintenance supervisor nodded. "They did that with the Temporaries. We used to receive and ship. Then it became profitable to have the customers take care of it, and suddenly shippers and receivers were working the lines in Maintenance."

Sofie let herself relax. It wasn't over by a long shot, but it finally felt like progress. The council needed to be formed from this group. Trust had to be built. And they didn't have months to figure things out. They didn't even have days.

"Unless anyone has something to add," she said, "we need to get started."

49

No one objected. Sofie tried not to feel a touch of victory. This wasn't a win, not even close. Their plan relied on too many assumptions. That they had time enough to put things in motion. That the Elites would understand the change in power. That anyone off the Mallet cared about what happened. That the Mallet was still profitable enough to tempt a buyer to negotiate. And that any negotiation would be in good faith.

Running through the problems in her head wouldn't help. Time to explain and hope these people agreed.

"We are all here to represent our areas of the Mallet. One of the first actions is to ensure that you are accepted in that role."

"Anyone still need to do that?" the Maintenance worker asked. Heads shook. "Unless you mean everyone will blindly follow, we're ready."

"I don't think we could trust it if anyone said they had that level of commitment." Sofie took a breath. Time to introduce the others and their roles. Not Nhu's betrayal. That was done, and the plan needed them to continue in the role of contact for the Elites. But every face on the screen was waiting for the name of the person who would save them.

"We all work together," she said. "I have a team with me. Two other detectives, who can work with the authorities." She indicated Amanda and Rick on the screen. "Some of you know Virgil Ten. He has already shown his talent as a leader."

Virgil nodded at the screen.

"Also, two former Executives," Sofie said. "Nhu Eckerman and Haadiya Rothwell. They will work as liaisons to the people off-station."

"How can we trust Executives?" the Maintenance worker asked. He was becoming the spokesperson for the group. Something Sofie would need to deal with if it became a problem. "They are probably working with the Elites."

Haadiya touched Sofie's arm, and she nodded for him to continue.

"I understand your reluctance," he said. "Let me remind you that the Elites left us behind when they fled. They showed no loyalty to us — not a surprise, but we take that as permission to act as we see fit. My colleagues are hiding. They are not equipped to deal with the violence. Eckerman and I are prepared to negotiate for the whole Mallet. It is to our benefit to change the power dynamic of the station. And we know how all the systems work."

"Pretty words," the worker said.

"Thank you." Haadiya smiled as though it was a compliment. "I mean every one of them."

"And that other Executive?" The man was not going to be easy to convince.

"I have a way of contacting the Elites." Nhu looked down at their lap, ending the questions.

"What do we need to do now?" Petra asked. "The medical teams are prepared for a rush of patients, but so far, we have seen minimal injuries. If that changes, we need to focus on our jobs, rather than our futures. I am prepared to allow Sofie to represent us."

"We need a list of demands," Sofie said. "And we need to understand which of the points are bargaining tools, and which are vital needs. We need to understand who will talk to the Elites. We need to do it fast."

"Are you sure it's the Elite families?" Petra asked. "If we are negotiating with the wrong people…"

"They are currently in control," Haadiya said. "The longer we take, the more competition we face."

"These private cops," the Maintenance worker said. "They hired by the Elites?"

That was a hard question to answer. Sofie agreed that they were probably on the Mallet to keep the violence from getting out of hand, and to delay enough for someone to prepare to take over, but that might not be the Elites.

"We have no way of knowing," Sofie said. "Our best guess is yes; the Elites are using them to keep us from seeing the truth. But they could be from one of the competing corporations that Haadiya mentioned. They arrived just before the Elites fled."

"How are we going to kick them off the Mallet?" the Manufacturing supervisor asked.

"It will be easy when we have power," Nhu answered before Sofie could speak. "But I think they will withdraw as soon as we appear to be winning. After all, they're expensive, and who wants to pay out for unsuccessful strategies?"

That elicited a chuckle from a few people.

"Are there any other questions?" Sofie asked. When no one responded, she said, "Then we should meet here again with our demands to prepare for negotiation. Is an hour enough?"

Sounds of banging came from the speakers. Three heads turned to look behind them.

"What was that?" Sofie asked. "Are you safe?"

"Those Ulindia assholes," the supervisor said. "We just ignore them for now, but they're getting more persistent. An hour is plenty. I have most of the demands now, but I will talk to a few people."

The screens went dark, and Sofie ended the call.

"We might need some guards," she said to Haadiya. "Are you trying to keep your secret identity hidden?"

"Yes, but if we need to protect people, I'll tell them. If I knew where they were, I would send guards now."

"Let's trust that they know what they are doing," she said. "We need to make our own list."

50

"How will we conduct negotiations with violence raging outside our door?" Nhu asked.

Sofie figured they were still looking for a way to shine for both the Elites and the new leaders of the Mallet, whoever that turned out to be.

"We start by doing what we asked the others to do: stay safe and make a list of demands," she said. "I'll try to talk to Llewelyn. He needs to know what we found out and what we plan. If only so he can be ready to take over when the Ulindia people leave."

"What do you want to add to the list?" Virgil asked.

"The same as everyone: the Mallet safe, and the caste system gone." She took a deep breath to clear all the problems running around in her mind. There were only two things she needed to pay attention to: saving the Mallet for the present and putting the future in place. "I guess I expect to be a cop when this is done."

"You try to get Llewelyn," Rick said. "I'll work on the list of demands. We only have an hour, remember?"

Sofie put her pad on the charger and went to the other

room. Now that Virgil was free, it was a good place to make a call, or just think without distractions for a minute.

She believed the Mallet could survive, but the future would be created out of the lowest and highest castes. The people in the middle, like the cops, doctors, and educators, wouldn't experience much change. The legal system was based on the desires of the Elites, so maybe a few new laws would be created and some struck off, but there would still be crime to investigate.

She activated her wrist comm and tapped in Llewelyn's private number. "We have news," she said when the tone on the messages prompted her to speak.

Sofie sat on the chair and stared at the wall. She wouldn't wait in the room for thirty minutes — the longest it would take for Llewelyn to check for messages. But a few minutes' peace to sort through everything that had happened and center herself for the next few hours wouldn't delay anything.

She'd woken up feeling healthy just under three days ago. For the first time in her life, she was free of worry about an attack. The riots and general unrest slowed them down, but suddenly they had a way out. One that could benefit everyone.

Her wrist comm buzzed. Llewelyn.

"What news?" he asked before she could say anything. "We're in the shit here, Sofie."

She blurted out every fact they'd accumulated, leaving out Nhu's involvement and Haadiya's secret identity. "So, you need to be ready to take the Mallet back from the Ulindia people."

"I agree that they will abandon us if you're successful," he said. "We'll be taking it back from our own residents if that happens. I have some news too. The riots are spreading.

It's like whoever was in charge is gone. The crowds are in the Support section and getting close to the Executive."

"Damaging the station?" If the violence was truly out of control, they were too late. "Fatalities?"

"Not yet," Llewelyn said. "I'm getting most of this secondhand. We've been confined to the station and our quarters. The only policing going on is coming from the Ulindia assholes."

"How long do you think before we can't stop it?" Sofie's mind began ticking off the tasks they needed to accomplish.

"That's my other news. I thought it was bad, but now, with what you told me, it might be the best news. The assholes are preparing to use harsh methods."

"Sedating the rioters?" It would buy her some time. "Or worse?"

"They'll flood an area with sedation. Bystanders, victims, people trying to calm the situation, will all pass out in a heap. Then they'll go in and beat the ones they think were rioting. I heard them say it didn't matter if they hit a civilian, being on the Mallet right now meant you were part of the problem."

Good and bad news all wrapped together.

"When will this start?"

"Probably a couple of hours," Llewelyn said. "While they prep, I can call our officers to get ready. How will I know when to act?"

"I'll make sure you know," Sofie said. "I'm not sure how. We have a lot to do in the next couple of hours."

She ended the call and rubbed her face in frustration. It was like a game where her opponent knew the rules and she didn't.

There were only ten minutes before the council got back together. Should she tell them about Ulindia's plans? No.

Everyone would be safe for long enough to fix the problem, so adding to their worries wasn't productive.

She joined the others in the room. One of the screens displayed a list of demands. Nothing she objected to, or thought was missing. "Amnesty?" she asked. "For everything that's happened in the last few days?"

"No, for any past misdeed," Haadiya said. "I have no wish to save the Mallet only to be imprisoned for running the dark streets."

"So everyone gets a new start?" The cop in her wanted to erase the word on the screen.

"How many of the people in prison are only there because the Elites made it impossible to survive without committing crimes?" Haadiya asked. "It's not like we'll be releasing murderers. Anyone who was found guilty of that is part of the compost system."

"And anyone who hasn't been caught is already free," she said. "Fine. Nhu, set up a meeting with the Ruiz Pratham for an hour from now. Don't tell her why, or who will be there."

51

The screens lit up as people joined the council meeting. It had only been an hour, but so much had changed. Sofie's confidence was beaten down and she couldn't let that show.

"Before we start, is everyone still safe?" she asked. If the private security team decided to impose their own version of order before the council could act, they had no hope.

"Yes, we are able to stay inside as long as we can communicate," the Maintenance worker said. "No one would be stupid enough to shut down the work in our section."

"Manufacturing is trickier," the supervisor said. "We mostly live in barracks. It is safe for now, no riots around us, so perhaps we are not attracting any attention."

"We've closed the clinic," Petra said. "I have someone watching to ensure any patients can be let in without giving access to the crowds. I do see more of that now, Sofie. I think the violence is spreading through the station."

"We'll work fast," Sofie said. "We have a meeting in an hour with one of the Elites. Someone who speaks for all of the families."

"It's too soon," the Maintenance worker said. "We haven't had a chance to refine our demands, or even think about everything we want."

Haadiya waved to Sofie off-screen to indicate he would answer. She nodded.

"There will never be enough time," he said, "but this meeting will not be the final one. Our goal is to get them to stop the violence and agree to our demand to negotiate the new contract."

The faces on the screen relaxed a bit with his words. Sofie would not have thought of those details. Of course, they couldn't get ready so quickly. But she would make sure the actual negotiations didn't drag on for months. For one, the grace period would run out and the Elites would probably return to the Mallet rather than lose it. That would take away any chance for negotiating a change.

"Let's look at the lists," Sofie said. The original purpose of the meeting was still critical. When that was done, she would tell them what she'd learned from Llewelyn. And they must decide on who would join the meeting with Lilianna Ruiz.

The left side of each screen filled with text.

"I'll collate it," Amanda said. "Just a second."

The lists flickered and then were replaced with what Amanda had combined. Ten points.

That's all it takes to save the Mallet? Ten changes.

"Is there anything to add?" she asked. "Or explain?"

She watched as all the attendees read the new points. If she could trust their body language, then this part of the meeting was about to come to an end.

"It's good," the supervisor said. "We didn't think of amnesty."

"There's a lot of detail to be worked out," the Maintenance worker said. "It's a good start, but I don't see anything on the list I'm willing to give up in negotiations."

Nhu glanced up from their screen. Sofie nodded, but this time with less confidence. She wasn't sure anymore if Nhu was out to sabotage everyone.

"Those items will be in the details. This is very good work. The list is short enough to make the Elites think it's simple, but it's also powerful."

It wasn't hard to get everyone to agree after that statement. And they all wanted to be in attendance, but only to observe. Leaving Sofie and her team to take any blame if the whole plan went wrong.

"Nhu will send you the meeting link," Sofie said. "Now I have news."

Faces tightened as Sofie passed on Llewelyn's news. Fear? Determination? She hoped for both.

"If we are successful, the security people will go," she said. "And their strategy is to cause confusion, not destroy anything."

"Is this just the Elites?" Petra asked.

Sofie looked to Nhu.

"We can't be sure," they said. "But it doesn't matter. When we are finished, anyone trying to take over will retreat. It will be too costly to continue."

They said the words with so much confidence that Sofie almost believed it was true. But there were no guarantees.

"Please watch your screens," Sofie said. "Call if you need help. We will see you in forty minutes."

She ended the call and waited for the screens to fill with images across the station.

"Virgil, can you try to warn your colleagues?" Amanda

asked. "The more we can get the word out, the fewer people will be on the streets."

Why didn't I think of that?

Virgil started tapping on the pad he'd borrowed from their supplies. He muttered as he worked, but only a few minutes later he looked up and shook his head. "No one is answering. I am afraid we are too late." He nodded toward the screens.

Images of crowds filled all the screens. The locations were all over the station; the only ones not affected were the two Temporaries and the Elite section. The reactions varied from section to section. In Maintenance, the crowds bloomed as people rushed to join the mayhem. In Manufacturing, the residents slipped away from the intruders as though distancing themselves from the chaos.

In Support, unit doors slammed down, but about half the people on the streets joined in with the shouted threats and arm waving.

"We can't let them defeat us now, just when we are about to win," Sofie said. "How can we calm this?"

"It would have to be from here," Rick said. "Station-wide alert?"

"On it," Amanda said. "It's going to take some time to hack access. Nhu, do you have codes?"

"No. It's automated and set to activate only when the station is in danger of fire, explosion, or something similar."

"But not riots?" Sofie asked.

"No." Nhu didn't add more.

"I'll do my best," Amanda said.

"Shit," Haadiya said. "There won't be anyone to hear a broadcast by the time we make it."

Sofie turned her attention back to the screens. Gray-clad

security personnel in gas masks were marching into the crowds, spraying a fog of sedation. The participants dropped as though dead. Within minutes no one was rioting — or moving.

52

"Is it worth sending a broadcast now?" Rick asked. "The people who need to hear it are unconscious. We don't know how long before they can think straight. And the Ulindia assholes might just lock them all up anyway."

Nothing is final, yet.

"What else can we do?" Sofie asked. "The plan is still the same, and we wanted our broadcast to calm things down. Well, they are calm. Amanda can concentrate on something else."

They had only a short time until the meeting with Lilianna Ruiz. Planning how to handle her was more important.

"No," Haadiya said. "There are other reasons to send our message out. Two off the top of my head."

Nhu was quiet. Sofie had the distinct feeling that they'd had the same thought as Haadiya but were holding it back for a power play later.

"We don't have time to guess," she said. "I already know

I'm not good at strategy, so don't feel like you have to protect me."

"The Ulindia team will hear the message, and perhaps it will convince them to leave a lost cause, or at least pause in their rush to subdue the station."

He scanned the screens and Sofie saw the rest of the team follow his gaze. The protesters were still heaped in the various squares, and the assholes were busy sending shocks through bodies that wouldn't feel pain. Doing damage for the fun of it?

"And the second reason?" Didn't he know how fast time was slipping away?

"Not everyone is lying in a pile. Your colleagues need to hear that we are about to win. The people who didn't join in the riots need to know they are safe."

Was that worth the risk that everyone who'd been sitting out the rebellion — because that's what it was — would start to take revenge? Or use the opportunity to loot, or... she didn't know what anyone would do, given the opportunity.

"We can ask them to be prepared to show strength in the negotiations," Nhu said, finally joining the conversation. "Solidarity is a powerful tool. Lilianna won't risk the Mallet being independent if it looks like a remote possibility."

Sofie kept her eyes on the screens. The sight of so much cruelty helped to focus her thoughts. The prods must have run out of charge because the security people were kicking a few of the bodies at the edge of the pile. She blinked away the fury that rose from her gut. The Mallet was a horrible place, but random violence like this was still a crime. Yes, it was because the Elites wanted residents working, but the reason didn't matter.

"Okay. Amanda, any idea how much longer you need?"

"I'm done," she said. "Finished it five minutes ago while everyone was still debating if it was worthwhile."

"Can you restore the controls when we finish?" Haadiya asked. "I don't like the idea that anyone can start broadcasting their message to the station. Imagine what the religious groups will do to our sanity with such access."

"I'll build stronger ones," Amanda said. "It's something we should add to a list of things to change when we're in charge."

The list didn't exist yet, and Sofie planned to be back on duty before anyone started deciding how the Mallet would be run.

"We have seven minutes," Nhu said. "Being late will only make Lilianna Ruiz stubborn. She still thinks the Elites are feared."

"Set up an observing attendee role and then we'll ask people to join our meeting." Sofie hoped more than a handful of faces would fill the screens. They needed numbers to create the image of solidarity.

"What do we tell them?" Amanda asked. "And who does the talking?"

Six minutes left and they still hadn't answered those questions for the meeting with the Ruiz Pratham.

"What we know about the situation; not about us, not where we are," Rick said. "Invite them to observe the meeting. Make no promises."

"And Rick does the talking," Sofie said. He had given a lot of thought to this and deserved the role. It would mean she could talk to the Ruiz Pratham when the meeting started.

Amanda handed Rick the pad she was using. "You're all set."

As she listened to Rick over the unit speakers, Sofie

watched the action on the screens. The Ulindia assholes stopped their abuse after the first few words. The assholes stepped to the edges of the pile of people as if they were afraid the sedation would be lifted by the truth. By the time Rick finished, the Ulindia team had retreated. The screens near the Temporaries showed them filing inside.

"Time," Nhu said.

Sofie sat and propped her pad on the stand. Lilianna did not appear; so she didn't think it was important enough to be prompt? Good, it gave Sofie time to think over her first words, the ones that would keep Lilianna listening rather than prompt her to end the conference.

"The observation link is live," Amanda said. "So far we have three thousand signed in."

Sofie smiled. That would get Lilianna's attention. "Can you display the number of attendees so she can't miss it?"

"Already happening. We're at five thousand six hundred and fifty."

Sofie checked screens again. People were entering the squares and doing their best to assist the protesters who were starting to recover.

53

Lilianna Ruiz's face flickered onto the center wall screen. Sofie checked the number of attendees displayed below her own image — ten thousand plus and ticking upward by the second.

As they'd agreed at the very last second, Nhu began the meeting. Their role was to keep Lilianna from ending the call before Sofie had a chance to speak.

"Nhu, what is this?" Lilianna said.

A good sign; she could have simply ended the call when she saw the number of people observing.

"Things have taken a turn," Nhu said. "The Mallet has organized a negotiating team. I strongly advise you to listen, Pratham. For the sake of all the Elites."

Sofie noticed that Nhu didn't use the word council. Good. Whatever body became the resident leaders of the Mallet, they should choose their own name. As long as it had nothing to do with the word *Elite*.

"And who is the spokesperson for this... team."

At least she didn't call us rabble or scum.

"I am," Sofie said. "Are you able to speak for the Elites?"

A smile crawled across Lilianna's face. "I am glad to see you in charge, Detective," she said. "I remind you of my title: Pratham. Please use it."

The meeting was already at the political stage. Sofie knew enough to keep her words soft and calm without being deferential. At this point, the Mallet was a blank page. Acknowledging her rank would give her power no one should have. Sofie tried to ignore the feeling she was performing for all the people they invited to observe because she couldn't try to please them now. She needed all her focus on this task.

"With respect, when you and the others abandoned the station, you forfeited your roles."

"So, you have seen the contract? Do I have Nhu Eckerman to... thank for that morsel?"

"It doesn't matter," Sofie said. "The station is quiet for now, and that is a result of our work, the people who stayed. We are here because we want to give you the first chance to negotiate with the residents."

"You don't want to take it for yourselves?" Lilianna showed shock. A Pratham showing any reaction was rare, and it gave Sofie hope.

"That is not possible," she said. "The Mallet needs the support of the customers. The takeover is inevitable. We prefer working with the former Elites. You have lived here; you've seen the pressures people are under. If you are not interested, we will move on. There is competition for ownership, after all. I think that gives us some weight."

Lilianna stared at Sofie's image without expression. She would see the number of observers. Was she calculating the odds of success if the Elites decided to forge ahead?

"I can speak to the other Prathams," she finally said. "I

am not prepared to negotiate now, and I make no promises about the future. What are your demands?"

This was what worried Sofie the most. How to get a level of confidence that Lilianna would negotiate in some form of good faith. The real work to solidify the deal wasn't her job. If someone appointed her, she'd dump her tracker and hide until the role was filled by someone more competent, or at least willing. This first step was hard enough. And knowing that almost a third of the Mallet was observing didn't make it any easier. She must set the tone for every meeting that came after this one. Any hint of capitulation would damage their chances at a fair deal. Each time Lilianna asked for something, Sofie was supposed to push back first. Giving the high-level demands was one of the goals, but she couldn't just hand them over.

"We are not prepared for detailed negotiation either," Sofie said. "We understand you need to know something of the cost of our offer, but if we can't be sure you will return to the table, we will open talks with another corporation."

"I believe we will work with you," Lilianna said after a pause. "I will recommend it, in fact. But if your demands are too high, the other families may choose to withdraw."

"You and your colleagues have formed a corporation to purchase the Mallet," Sofie said. "Who is selling it if not the people here?"

"True, but Sofie, don't forget the Elites are also people who lived on the Mallet."

"And no longer do," Sofie said. "Who did you expect to pay for our services?" Now that she'd thought of the question, Sofie wanted an answer. She and her team had been so busy trying to solve all the problems, she hadn't even thought enough to ask it. This meeting had made her realize that there could be a hidden competitor.

Lilianna turned to someone out of range of the camera. She nodded and then said, "There is a clause in the contract. With enough time, Nhu or any other Executive would have found it. We would pay our clients a substantial fine. Buying the Mallet is about turning the fine into a purchase price. Does that answer your question?"

"Who is with you?" Sofie asked.

"Representatives of our new corporation," Lilianna said.

"Enough to agree to negotiate in good faith with us?"

"Well caught, Detective. Yes." Lilianna seemed proud of Sofie for working it out.

"You have ten minutes to discuss with them and then we need an answer," Sofie said.

Lilianna's image froze on the screen as she placed the meeting on hold.

"Well done," Haadiya said.

Sofie took in a breath and blew out the tension she'd been holding through the discussion. "I have no idea what to do if she comes back with a no."

"She won't," Nhu said. "Do not give any names to her, but say the next meeting will be with an elected council. Don't let her delay too long. Today, if possible, tomorrow at the latest. We can't let them regroup and start the mess again."

Now the balance of power had shifted to the residents, and Nhu was happy to help. Sofie didn't think it was for the benefit of anyone but Nhu Eckerman. But the advice was good.

"Just tell them the high points," Amanda said. "Don't ask what they want. Treat this like a sale with a bit of haggling on price, not a negotiation. They are much better at taking advantage than you."

The screen with Lilianna's image flickered and then showed her live.

"Are you ready?" Sofie asked. "Or do we move on?"

"So impatient," Lilianna said with a smile. Sofie was getting sick of the patronizing tone. "We agree that our best and fastest solution is to negotiate with you. This will cost the families the price of the fine, but that is insignificant in view of the future income."

"At the high level, we want equality for the residents, no more castes. Amnesty for any crimes committed before and during the recent upheaval. Rule of the Mallet is in the hands of a representative council."

"Is that all?" Lilianna asked.

"The details will be worked out by the elected representatives. If you agree in principle, we are prepared to set the next session." Could the negotiating team be selected fast enough for a meeting today? They would have to be. "In three hours?"

Lilianna hadn't been expecting that. She opened her mouth but didn't speak. Someone must have spoken to her off-screen. She turned and frowned at them, then looked back to the camera. "That is fast, but we can be prepared if you can. Send me the link, and I will invite the people who can make decisions." She left the meeting before Sofie could speak.

"I am not going to be elected to negotiate." Sofie wanted the words to be heard by everyone in attendance so she could be free of pressure to change her mind.

"I can coordinate," Amanda said. "We need a small team. There are nine families; if we have ten people, it should show strength."

Sofie ended the meeting.

"I'm going to get things started up again," Sofie said. "Rick? Are you coming?"

54

Hard to believe it had only been five days since the end of the riots. The Ulindia team hadn't waited for orders — or they had standing orders to leave under specific conditions. Their retreat to the Temporaries didn't even pause long enough for them to take a breath. They filed into waiting shuttles and cleared Mallet space in minutes.

While Sofie spoke to Lilianna, Llewelyn had sent the entire police force out to assist the protesters with clearing the squares and getting medical attention where needed.

By the start of the next shift, the Mallet was back to normal operations. Changes would come, Sofie knew, but it would take time for them to show. She'd happily taken two days to recover and let others do the work to clean up the mess.

The council elections took half an hour; she suspected the names were already picked before the call. Haadiya was placed as the head, probably based on his ability to run the dark streets. He'd told his secret as soon as the amnesty agreement was in place with the former Elite families. Nhu was back in their old role, just reporting to a council rather than a family. Their true role in the chaos was still a secret.

Sofie was on her way to attend the first regular council meeting. As a guest, not a participant. Her wrist comm buzzed. Torque.

"You're back?" she asked.

"Got here yesterday. Took a while to set up again. Weird, it's like nothing happened here. How's the rest of the station?"

"A bit bruised, but fine." She wanted to divert from her course and join Torque for a drink at one of his favorite bars. But she'd promised to attend the meeting and it was in the Support section, a long way from the outgoing Temps. "Meet you later for a catch-up?"

"Always ready to chat," he said.

She ended the call and stood looking at the unit door to the newly appointed council meeting space. The people inside had a hard job ahead to transition the Mallet from what it was to what everyone wanted. The caste system wouldn't disappear just because someone said it no longer existed. The work was still the same, and the sections of the Mallet were still called by their caste names. She didn't regret refusing a role, although Haadiya had lobbied hard for her to join the council.

She held her card to the contact pad and waited for the small door to open.

The room inside must have been a lecture hall before. It had tiered seating facing a long table at the front of the room, where a professor would normally stand. Ten seats were set around the table. This is where the council would sit. Screens lined the wall behind the table. It was a good design for participation.

"Like it?" Haadiya asked. He'd stepped through the entrance without her noticing.

"It gives the impression the council is open to listening. Is that real?" She hoped it was.

"We'll only know that as time passes," he said. "This is the first meeting. It's being broadcast. You are the only guest this time. Other than the media representatives, that is."

"Please tell me this isn't an ambush," Sofie said.

"No. We've heard you loud and clear. You won't be asked to sit on the council. No medals. I thought you would be interested in seeing us at work."

"Where do I sit?" Sofie asked. If Haadiya was just being considerate, maybe she should try to believe it.

"We'd like you in the front. We may need you to answer some questions about what happened. Nothing hard. I promise."

"How do you decide anything without an odd number?" She nodded to the ten chairs. "You're going to get bogged down if someone can't break a tied vote."

"It's not that simple," he said with a laugh. "If only it was down to five yes and five no. We keep getting stuck trying to make each decision into one simple point, so we don't have multiple blocs. It hasn't worked so far, but I guess it shouldn't be easy to build a fair future, right?"

"At least you got far enough to make a deal with the Elites, and one that keeps their entitled asses off the station."

"That's mainly the agenda today. We all agreed that the terms should be public. Come, I'll introduce you before we start."

· · ·

SOFIE SIPPED HER STIM-JUICE. The broadcast was more interesting than she expected. Having been through the action, she thought it would be dull, but it wasn't just facts and contract reading. There were stories from residents. Explanations from council members about their thinking. Not exactly entertaining, but enough to keep people focused.

There were two contracts. The one between the Mallet as represented by the council and the former Elites was simple. The Elites held no power over the operation of the Mallet. Their role was to maintain relationships with customers. If the Mallet became unprofitable, the residents would be relocated. The first month's profit would be accepted as payment for all outstanding debts. The Mallet residents were free to leave, and new workers didn't arrive with crippling debt.

The council rules were less clear but talked of equality and participation. The clause that gave Sofie hope was the guarantee of elections every five years. It would be harder for any one person to accumulate enough power to take control if they were required to campaign.

THE MEETING TOOK AN HOUR; long enough to get the message across, short enough that no worker would be forced to miss the news.

"Well?" Haadiya asked as the council and media packed up. "Is this what you expected?"

"A good start," she said. "We'll see how things shake out."

"I'll do my best," he said. "But we're people, Sofie, not saints."

"Are you ready?" Nhu asked Haadiya as they walked over. "The Ruiz quarters are cleared out for you to move in."

"You're moving to the Elite section?" Sofie asked.

"Don't worry, it only means the council will be close together," Nhu said. "It's the only area we could use without disturbing other residents."

Sofie bit back the words that jumped to mind. She nodded and walked away. Those quarters could have been broken up to make life easier on everyone. This was the cost of her not joining the council. She had no right to challenge their decisions. What surprised her was the feeling of betrayal. She didn't think she'd held so much hope things would change.

WANT MORE?

Use the QR code to find more thrilling science fiction books by P A Wilson.

If you enjoyed reading Red Lined, please consider helping other readers to find the story by leaving a review.

FREE EBOOK

Claim your copy of Running the Game when you use the
QR code below to sign up for my newsletter and cheer on
Pen as she vies for a commission in the military.

ALSO BY PA WILSON

For more books by P A Wilson

Use the QR code below or go to pawilson.ca

ABOUT THE AUTHOR

Perry Wilson is a Canadian author based in Vancouver, BC who has big ideas and an itch to tell stories. Having spent some time on university, a career, and life in general, she returned to writing in 2008 and hasn't looked back since (well, maybe a little, but only while parallel parking).

She is a member of the Vancouver Writers Social Group, The Royal City Literary Arts Society, and The Surrey Writing Workshop. Perry has self-published several novels. She writes the Madeline Journeys, a fantasy series about a high-powered lawyer who finds herself trapped in a magical world, the Quinn Larson Quests, which follows the adventures of a wizard named Quinn who must contend with volatile fae in the heart of Vancouver, and the Charity Deacon Investigations, a mystery thriller series about a private eye who tends to fall into serious trouble with her cases, and The Riverton Romances, a series based in a small town in Oregon, one of her favorite states. Her stand-alone novels are Breaking the Bonds, Closing the Circle, and The Dragon at The Edge of The Map.

For more information
www.pawilson.ca
pawilson@pawilson.ca

ACKNOWLEDGMENTS

People think that the process of writing is solitary. That's not the case for me. I have help from so many people it would be hard to acknowledge everyone, but I'll give it a try.

The support and inspiration I get from my writer's groups is incalculable. The Vancouver Writers Social Group opens my mind to other ways of telling a story. The Royal City Literary Arts Society gives me the opportunity to meet and share with other writers who have more knowledge than I do. The Other 11 Months group is where I learn about getting the words on the page. And my critique group who helps me find the best parts of the story I want to tell. Thanks to all of the members of these great groups.

Last of all, but definitely a huge part of the process, my beta readers. These are the people who love stories and are willing, and more than able, to tell me if my finished story is ready for you, my readers.